"Let's make a deal,"
he whispered softly.

Kate didn't know if she was capable of doing anything that rational at the moment.

"Let's call a truce, Katie. Let's be partners, or co-conspirators, or whatever you want to call it. Let's try to get along."

She felt feverish. His lips had left her ear and were trailing down the side of her neck, licking and nibbling and leaving fiery imprints behind. "What does it involve?" she barely managed to say.

He pulled away from her for a few seconds, only enough time for her to see the devilish gleam in his eyes. "Something along these lines," he said as he pressed his lips against hers and started to kiss her . . .

Dear Reader:

We're celebrating SECOND CHANCE AT LOVE's third birthday with a new cover format! I'm sure you had no trouble recognizing our traditional butterfly logo and distinctive SECOND CHANCE AT LOVE type. But you probably also noticed that the cover artwork is considerably larger than before. We're thrilled with the new look, and we hope you are, too!

In a sense, our new cover treatment reflects what's been happening *inside* SECOND CHANCE AT LOVE books. We're constantly striving to bring you fresh and original romances with unexpected twists and delightful surprises. We introduce promising new writers on a regular basis. And we aim for variety by publishing some romances that are funny, some that are poignant, some that are "traditional," and some that take an entirely new approach. SECOND CHANCE AT LOVE is constantly evolving to meet your need for "something new" in your romance reading.

At the same time, we *haven't* changed the successful editorial concept behind each SECOND CHANCE AT LOVE romance. And we've consistently maintained a reputation for being a line of the highest quality.

So, just like the new covers, SECOND CHANCE AT LOVE romances are satisfyingly familiar—yet excitingly different—and better than ever!

Happy reading,

Ellen Edwards

Ellen Edwards, Senior Editor
SECOND CHANCE AT LOVE
The Berkley Publishing Group
200 Madison Avenue
New York, N.Y. 10016

P.S.   Do you receive our SECOND CHANCE AT LOVE and TO HAVE AND TO HOLD newsletter? If not, be sure to fill out the coupon in the back of this book, and we'll send you the newsletter free of charge four times a year.

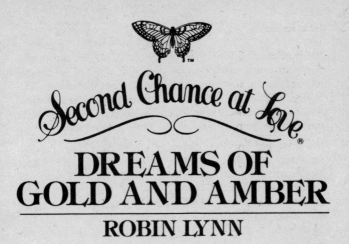

Second Chance at Love ®

DREAMS OF GOLD AND AMBER

ROBIN LYNN

SECOND CHANCE AT LOVE
BOOK

For Kathy

First edition published August 1984

First printing

"Second Chance at Love" and the butterfly emblem are trademarks
belonging to Jove Publications, Inc.

Printed in the United States of America

Second Chance at Love books are published by
The Berkley Publishing Group
200 Madison Avenue, New York, NY 10016

Chapter 1

KATE BURNHAM ALMOST stabbed a celery stick into the onion dip, then changed her mind and crunched into the vegetable in its naked state. From her vantage point at the buffet table set up in a secluded corner of the gallery, Kate's wide gray eyes surveyed the crowd. It wasn't a bad turnout for the Havenport College Art Museum's first fall exhibition. The usual number of students milled about, more interested in the free wine than the exquisite sixteenth-century Italian prints on the walls, and the trustees and their wives performed their customary elegant social ballet: a kiss here, a peck there, handshakes for some and smiles for all. Brushing aside the golden-red bangs that just touched her eyebrows, Kate watched as Helen Drummond, the petite but dynamic curator of Italian art, accepted congratulations on her beautifully presented show.

Kate smoothed her charcoal-colored pleated skirt over hips that were just a trifle too curvaceous to be fashionable. Ruefully, she realized that her palms were moist with nervous sweat as she observed Helen mixing and mingling with her well-wishers. A month from now, Kate would be opening her own exhibition, on abstract expressionism, and she was terrified she was going to fall flat on her face with it.

Kate had expected that the director of the museum, Alexander Jensen, would cover all the costs of the show—costs that could be formidably high when you took into account insurance for all the loaned works, shipping charges, and the reframing and conservation of some of the canvases. But Jensen hated the abstract expressionists—"messy painters" he'd called them yesterday when he had told her he'd only give her a minimal amount toward her expenses and suggested that she be very resourceful and find the rest of the money elsewhere. It had been quite a jolt.

"Excuse me." A deep, unfamiliar male voice came from behind her and interrupted her anxious thoughts. Kate felt an arm brush lightly against her and, looking down, saw a well-manicured hand below the cuff of a tweed jacket plunge a carrot stick into the dip bowl. Her gaze followed the hand up from the bowl, noticing the conservative, well-cut trousers that covered the man's husky frame. She watched in fascination as the carrot traveled in front of his broad chest, which was clad in a tweed jacket and a button-down shirt; then she nearly choked in surprise as a big glob of the dip slipped off the carrot and landed with a noisy plop on the linen tablecloth.

Kate had been brought up to believe that when in the company of someone who has made a faux pas, the gracious thing to do is cover up for them immediately. And so, without even thinking, she pressed her hand against the glass edge of the dip bowl and casually slid it over the stain, as if nothing out of the ordinary had happened. Then she looked up to see for whom she'd done the favor.

The first thing she noticed was his eyes. They weren't brown and they weren't green but almost gold; they were bright and deep and rich in color, and were surrounded by eyelashes that were just as lustrous and fine. His eyes had an extraordinary quality of penetration in their ebony centers, and they seemed to be taking her in with an intense and curious scrutiny, as if he were sizing her up and coming to a final conclusion about her in one long and almost arrogant glance. But there was no arrogance in the rest of his face. High, wide cheekbones angled downward to a jaw that was square and strong; the broad forehead was brushed with vigorously wavy hair the color of a chestnut stallion. His mouth was wide and mobile, and his lips turned up at their corners as if he were about to laugh.

"Thank you," he said softly as he pressed her arm lightly with his hand.

She trembled slightly while he continued to stare into her eyes, probing them. Kate began to suspect that he was deliberately trying to draw her in and engulf her with his compelling golden gaze. She felt as if she'd shrunk and fallen into a pot of honey: sticky and sweet and helpless.

She had heard about eyes that hypnotized, but never having experienced them before, she had attributed such descriptions to overly romantic imaginations. Yet, here she was, spellbound by this man's golden gaze and hoping she didn't look as goony-eyed as she felt.

"You're welcome," Kate replied, slightly out of breath, even though she had been standing in the same place for quite a while.

Suddenly, Helen appeared in front of the table and Kate decided to start a conversation with her fellow curator, ignoring the man at her side and hoping that he'd go away. There was no place in her life for trembling knees and golden glances. Hadn't her experience in Dallas taught her that?

She edged away from the stranger to the far end of the table, and Helen followed. From the corner of her eye, Kate could see him giving her a perplexed look.

"Well, what do you think?" Helen asked, her hazel eyes snapping excitedly in her small, heart-shaped face.

"Helen, it's a beautiful show," Kate said sincerely. It really is, Kate thought to herself; if only mine can be this good.

Helen smiled. "Thanks. Other curators' opinions are what really matter to me. No one else knows all the work that goes into an exhibition. But you're just getting into gear on yours, aren't you?"

"Yes." Kate paused while she noticed Mr. Golden Gaze shaking hands with a distinguished-looking man in a gray suit. She felt safe now from further interruption, so she plunged right into the questions she had for Helen.

"Helen, I need some advice." She ran a hand nervously through her fine, shoulder-length hair.

"Sure, what is it?"

"Well, everyone knows you're a whiz at raising funds for your shows. How did you do this one?" Kate asked with a serious look.

Helen laughed softly. "I take it you're a little short on funds for yours."

"Short would mean I have something. Helen, all I've got is a promise from Jensen that the floors will be polished, and that's only because my show just happens to fall right after the monthly polishing." She was exaggerating a bit, but Helen would know she wasn't that far off the mark.

"Alex isn't overly fond of abstract expressionists, is he?"

"That's putting it politely," Kate said wryly. "But tell me, Helen, where did you get the money for *your* show?"

"Well, luckily for me, some funds came through that President Simpson had promised me before he left."

Kate sighed. "I doubt if I'd have much success appealing to the new president, this Radley Davis character. From the letter he published in the student newspaper yesterday, he sounds as if he thinks the arts are a big waste of time." Kate's voice had risen and she saw the man at the end of the table look over at her sharply. "According to President Davis, we have to 'become self-sufficient or perish.'" Kate quoted Davis with a large dose of pomposity.

"I feel sorry for the man," Helen said.

"Sorry!" Kate exclaimed indignantly. "Helen, he's practically written our death warrant—and you feel sorry for him?" She snuck a peek toward the end of the table again. Drat, he was still there.

"Kate, you're a relative newcomer here at Havenport, so you don't really know what he's just walked into. Harold Simpson was a terrific educator, but he was a terrible businessman. The college budget has been running in the red for years. Now they've brought in this Davis fellow to straighten the mess out, because he has a lot of business experience. I don't envy him. It's not a good time for small private colleges, and Davis has quite a job ahead of him."

"And so do I, with a miser for a president," Kate said, and punctuated it with a nervous laugh. "Any suggestions?"

Helen pondered Kate's question for a moment. Then something seemed to click in her mind, because her face broke into a wide smile.

"I know someone who might want to help you. He's a trustee of the museum who used to collect abstract expressionists in the fifties. Call me tomorrow and I'll give you his phone number. You can call him."

"But what do I say to him?" Kate blurted out before she could stop herself.

Helen looked at her, aghast. "Kate Burnham, are you telling me that you've never done this kind of thing before?"

"This is my first show here," Kate reminded her. Funds for exhibitions had never been a problem in Dallas, thanks to David Atwood, the director of the college museum and the man she had thought she loved. David had made sure that Kate always had more than enough money for the shows she mounted with his assistance—until the last one, and then he had made sure it was a disaster. But now that she was at Havenport, whether or not she was a success or a failure rested only on her shoulders. It was a little frightening, but she supposed that was the price you paid for devoting yourself totally to your work. If you failed professionally, then you failed personally, too. There was nothing to fall back on for comfort.

"Well, it won't be a problem. You wouldn't be here if we hadn't thought you were going to be a crack fund-raiser. I was on the search committee that hired you, and believe me, the competition was stiff. You won hands down. Everyone was impressed by your drive and your enthusiasm and your intelligence, Kate, and that's the truth."

Kate began to blush. She had never been good at responding to compliments, especially when they were as freely given and sincere as Helen's. It was wonderful to have her support.

"Thank you," she said slowly, and then made a joke to smooth over her awkwardness. "I thought I was coming to the land of milk and honey here. I thought money was just going to shower down and all I'd have to do was pick it up."

"Surprise!" Helen touched her arm, then pressed it comfortingly. "Perk up, Kate. You'll be a whiz. The secret's in the smile, really. Here, watch me."

Helen was engaged in showing Kate her surefire smile tactic when Kate began to feel the presence of someone hovering near them. It was Mr. Golden Gaze, the dip-dripper himself. She'd hoped he'd disappear, but he hadn't.

"Hello again," he interrupted them jovially.

Helen looked up quickly and then shot Kate a questioning look, as if she could give her a clue as to who the man might be, but Kate gave an impatient shrug of her shoulders to indicate that she had no idea.

"You were very kind to me before," he said, looking at Kate. He turned to Helen. "I dripped some onion dip on the tablecloth and she covered it up with the dip bowl so no one would know what a social misfit I was. Wasn't that nice?" He directed his radiant gaze at Kate.

"It was either that or dump the rest of the bowl

onto the table," Kate replied ungraciously. What was it about him that could elicit such a bad-tempered reply from her?

An awkward silence began to grow among the three of them. Kate picked an imaginary piece of lint off her skirt and straightened the cuffs on her silk blouse uneasily. Helen must be wondering what this is all about, she thought, but she had no way of telling her.

"It's a very good show," the man said. Kate supposed he thought there was nothing in that statement that she could object to.

"Helen"—Kate indicated Helen with a flick of her hand—"will be happy to hear that. She's the curator."

"Oh." His features became animated. "You're Helen Drummond, then?"

Helen held out her hand and shook his in a friendly fashion. "Yes. I'm glad you're enjoying the exhibit."

"And I'm glad I got to meet the curator."

He smiled again and his smile seemed to convey a great deal of energy and zest. Then he turned to Kate with a questioning look in his amber eyes.

"Kate Burnham." Kate held out her hand to him reluctantly and he enfolded it in a broad, warm palm.

"Sam. I'm a friend of one of the trustees." Was she imagining it, or did he seem to give her hand an extra, teasing squeeze just before she withdrew it from his? She trembled ever so slightly again. He was gazing into her eyes, waiting, perhaps, for some kind of reaction, but Kate kept her face expressionless.

"Are you a curator here too?"

"Yes. American arts," she answered.

"How patriotic," he said with just a little too much enthusiasm.

"Yes," she replied. "It makes the Fourth of July so exciting."

Helen looked at her and Kate could detect puzzlement in her eyes. Obviously, Helen couldn't figure out why Kate was being so rude to the man, and to be truthful, neither could Kate.

"I hear the new president is going to stop by soon," Sam said, changing the subject.

"That's quite an honor," Helen said kindly, trying to smooth over the tension that had developed between Kate and Sam. "I'd like to meet him."

"He's very interested in art," Sam said.

Kate stared at him suspiciously. How much of her conversation with Helen had he overheard? Was he deliberately trying to bait her? "I'm surprised to hear you say that," she said.

"Oh?" Sam was staring at her with his golden eyes again. "Why do you say that?"

From the look on Helen's face, Kate could see her acute uneasiness about the direction in which the conversation was going. But art was something Kate cared about passionately, and it was impossible for her to hold her tongue.

"Judging from his letter in yesterday's paper, he doesn't seem to give a darn for the arts," Kate said firmly.

"Really? What did the letter say?" Sam crossed his arms over his broad chest and rested his weight on his left leg. Kate watched uneasily as the firm outline of his thigh pressed against the flannel of his trousers.

"It said that the arts organizations of Havenport were going to have to become self-supporting or perish. That doesn't seem sympathetic to this museum—

in fact, it sounds like a threat." She shot him a quick glance to see what his reaction was, and she suddenly realized that he wasn't interested in what she had to say: He was interested in her! That wasn't something she wanted to encourage. She decided to quash his interest, and the only way she could think of doing so was by being disagreeable. "I think President Davis has no understanding of the arts. No doubt he's just a boring businessman who thinks art is a frivolous accessory to education, and in my opinion he couldn't be more wrong."

Sam looked at her appraisingly. "Perhaps you're jumping to conclusions. Have you met the man?"

He had her there. "No, but I don't see how that matters. I know what he says, and he's wrongheaded as far as I'm concerned. I think the trustees of the museum should know about it."

Sam laughed. "Is that a hint? Am I supposed to pass your opinion on to my friend?"

Had he caught on to her game? Was he calling her bluff? She decided to call his. "That's up to you."

"Thank you, Curator Kate. I don't respond well to demands."

He was annoyingly jovial. But beneath his joking tone Kate could sense a will that was just as strong as her own.

"I'm not a demanding woman, just a forthright one," she retorted.

"I won't deny that." He paused. "But you may have a point. Art is important. Have you thought of telling the president how you feel?"

He had caught on, she was sure of that, and now he was baiting her.

"I'm sure he'd like to hear your views," he continued. "A president needs to know how the people of his college feel. Why not tell him?"

"I just may do that," she said firmly.

There was a short, tense silence, and then Sam changed the subject. "Do you have any exhibits in the works yourself?" he asked politely.

"I'm planning a show on abstract expressionism next month," Kate replied.

"I'm sure it will be . . ." he paused dramatically for emphasis, ". . . invigorating."

"At least." Why did she feel as if she had to top everything he said? How had she gotten into this kind of interaction so quickly with Sam what's-his-name?

A silence developed again. Helen twitched nervously and then spoke up.

"Kate, there's something I have to show you. It's in my coat. Will you excuse us, please?" She nodded toward Sam.

Helen must have had enough of the tension, Kate realized instantly, for her to make such an obvious attempt at a getaway.

"Certainly." Sam gave Kate one last golden glance and then left them with long, vigorous strides.

Kate and Helen swiftly made their way to the cloakroom. As soon as they got there, Helen turned and began to interrogate her.

"Kate Burnham, why were you so rude to that man? Why in heaven's name did you say some of the things you did? You don't even know who he is." Helen's face showed concern.

"I know, I know." Sam was gone and it seemed as if he had taken her agitation with him. Now she was left with the sinking feeling that she had made a horrible fool of herself.

Helen must have sensed Kate's remorse, for she patted her on the arm. "Don't worry about it, Kate. You're under a lot of pressure. It's got to come out somewhere. Better on a perfect stranger than someone with whom it could do some real harm."

Kate appreciated her friend's attempt to make her feel better. "Like the infamous Radley Davis?"

"You wouldn't dream..." Helen looked at her, wide-eyed.

"No, I'm just kidding," Kate said, but she wasn't sure if she meant it or not. "Helen, you'd better get back in there. I've taken up too much of your time already."

"There are a few people I still have to talk to— thank, mostly. Do you want me to try to smooth things over with Sam if I talk to him again?"

"I appreciate the offer but perhaps it would be better if we all just forgot that it happened."

"All right. Talk to you tomorrow. I've got that trustee's number for you, remember?"

How kind of Helen to part with a reminder that she knew someone who might be able to help her out. Kate smiled at the older woman's back as she headed into the gallery. She was lucky to have Helen as a colleague and a friend.

Kate turned to the coats hanging on the rack and began to search through them haphazardly to find her own. She couldn't remember where she had put it. Was her mind going or did it just feel that way? Finally she found her coat, pulled it off the hook and proceeded to put her right arm through the left armhole. Standing there with the beginnings of a coat on back-wards, she suddenly began to laugh. If the arms were a little longer and could wrap around the back, she'd be enclosed in something approximating a strait-jacket, and that seemed completely apropos of her state of mind tonight.

"Wrap me up and cart me off to the loony bin," she mumbled to herself. Feeling about to drown in a man's gaze, trembling at his touch, feasting on the sight of his muscles straining against the cloth that covered them—those were feelings that she could only shake her head in wonderment at. She'd thought she was finally immune to that kind of thing.

As she left the museum Kate caught a quick glimpse of herself in the glass of the door. She looked earnest and determined, not the kind of woman who would respond to ardor in a man's eyes. In a flash of insight Kate saw herself twenty years in the future, alone in a room filled with books, a spinster. Was that what she really wanted?

She shrugged and headed down the stairs into the autumn twilight. Whether or not she wanted it was beside the point. Her career was the only thing she had, and it would have to be enough. Blast Mr. Golden Gaze for making her want more.

Chapter 2

"MORNING, KATE."

Kate had just climbed the steps to her office and entered the little reception area, which contained a few chairs, a round table covered with art magazines, and the desk of her curatorial assistant, Jane Fedders. Jane was already hard at work on some loan forms for the paintings Kate was borrowing from other institutions for her show, but looked up to greet Kate.

"Hi, Jane." Jane looked bright-eyed and bushy-tailed this morning, and Kate envied her energy. She hadn't slept well the night before. Worry and concern about her run-in with Sam and the problems with the funding of her exhibition had kept her awake until the wee hours. Her nerves felt very shaky.

"Is there any coffee?" she asked Jane.

"Lots. I just made a pot."

Kate headed back to the small kitchen at the back of the hall. She poured herself a mug of coffee, thinned it with a healthy dollop of milk, and then walked back to her office, gulping it down. She threw her briefcase of books and papers on her desk and then picked up the phone. She had to talk to Alexander Jensen this morning and she figured she'd catch him before he got involved with anything else. When she got Alex on the line, he told her to come up at eleven-thirty; he had some odds and ends to take care of first.

"Uh-oh." Kate heard Jane talking to herself outside her office, then the assistant poked her head in the door. "Care to see President Davis's latest?" She held up the morning's student newspaper.

"Oh, no. Not another!"

"Looks even worse than the last," Jane warned.

"Let me have a look. I'm going to make an appointment with him for this afternoon, if he'll see me, and I may as well know what I'm up against." Jane tossed the paper on Kate's desk.

Kate pulled it over, opened it up, and picked up her coffee, taking a quick, anxious sip. Radley Davis's new "Letter to Students, Staff, and Faculty" was set smack dab in the center of the front page, prominent and unavoidable.

Kate began to skim. At first it looked the same as yesterday's missive: serious financial straits...new policies of fuel and energy conservation... considering cutting down on library hours... And then Kate hit the real corker. Davis's final paragraph began with his most inflammatory statement yet:

To put it bluntly, and in terms rarely used in the hallowed halls of academia, anyone with half a brain must find it evident that organizations that cater to the arts must begin to be self-supporting. This college can no longer afford to pay for special events that appeal only to the knowledgeable elite. This means that the Drama Society, the Symphony, the Literary Quarterly, and the Art Museum will have to pay their own way. Surely they have patrons who will help them along in their efforts.

Kate threw down the paper. He'd finally come out and said it. He was cutting the museum off without a penny, and in the most insulting terms. "Anyone with half a brain" indeed! She had much more than half a brain, and it wasn't evident to her that arts organizations had to become self-supporting. That kind of attitude could be evident only to a man who had no interest in the arts in the first place. Davis was jeopardizing the education of the students at Havenport just because he had some kind of bug in his brain about art, literature, music, and drama. Kate couldn't stand it any longer. She'd have to respond to his ridiculous letter.

She reached for her telephone and dialed the president's office. While she waited for the connection to click into operation, she considered the options before her. She could speak with President Davis over the phone and tell him exactly how she felt about his new policies, but did she really want to jeopardize her position at the museum? If Davis was as hellbent as he seemed to be to cut off the museum completely, he might consider getting rid of a curator or two, a logical next step. Losing her job was not a viable option.

An older female voice answered the phone. "President Davis's office."

In a split second Kate made her decision. She'd ask for an appointment that afternoon and thus have the rest of the morning and lunchtime to figure out her strategy. The president's secretary told her that he could squeeze her in at one o'clock. Kate hung up the phone and then sat staring into space for several minutes.

She knew that there was no use telling President Davis bluntly what she thought about his new policies. If he knew how vehemently opposed to them she was, he certainly wouldn't be likely to funnel any money her way for the exhibition. For half a second she almost wished she were back in Dallas, where she had never had to think about these kinds of things because David had done all the thinking for her. But what kind of life was that? It was only half a life, really. Now she had to make her own life with her own decisions.

She grabbed a piece of paper out of her paper bin and stuffed it into her typewriter. If she couldn't tell President Davis face-to-face what she thought about his letter, she could always answer him with her own letter, an anonymous one, in the "Letters to the Editor" section of the student newspaper. All the letters were anonymous. It was the paper's policy to encourage freedom of speech. Kate was all for freedom. She began to type and the words just seemed to stream out effortlessly.

To the Editor:

President Davis's recent letter to the students, faculty, and staff of Havenport College regarding his new austerity program points the way, but it just doesn't go far enough. Therefore, I'd like to make several more suggestions for economizing at the college.

Perhaps we should consider doing away with

electricity completely. If candles and studying by firelight were good enough for Abraham Lincoln, why should it be beyond the reach of our great American college? I suggest that all classes during the evening hours be conducted by candlelight. Dinner in the dining hall would also be lovely in the glow of flickering tapers. Perhaps then it wouldn't be so obvious that the quality of the food being served was taking a drastic nosedive. In fact, campus dining halls seem to me to be a money-wasting luxury that perhaps the students of Havenport could do without. Let them fend for themselves. It will build character.

As far as cutting down on the consumption of fuel goes, I suggest that we just do away with central heating altogether. We should encourage students to carry hand warmers, make better use of the fireplaces Havenport has so generously provided in some of their living quarters, and make it mandatory to do vigorous calisthenics between classes to raise the body temperature. Healthy bodies make for healthy minds.

I agree with the president's policy of cutting down on student activities. Students are here to learn, not indulge in hedonistic pursuits, like listening to symphonies, or going to art museums, which we all know by now are merely temples of elitism.

I applaud President Davis's efforts to return this august college to the policies of its Puritan forebears. It doesn't take a person with less than half a brain to realize that things were getting totally out of hand here.

P.S. I suggest that all faculty members be re-
quested to bring their own tea bags to faculty
teas.

Kate pulled her letter out of the typewriter with a
gleefully satisfied flourish. That certainly told him!
She was especially pleased with the way she'd managed to say exactly what she thought of his hare-
brained ideas while pretending to compliment him on
them. Now all she had to do was figure out a pen
name. She pondered for half a minute, then snapped
her fingers. She popped the paper back in and tapped
out dramatically:

Most sincerely yours,

More Than Half a Brain

That should do it. That should do it fine! She folded
the letter, stuffed it into a campus-mail envelope, and
scrawled *The Havenport Observer* across the front.

She was heading out the door to go to the college
post office before she lost the courage of her convic-
tions when her phone rang. She motioned to Jane to
answer it.

Jane put the caller on hold after she'd found out
who it was.

"Helen," she announced.

"I'll call her back later."

Kate ran down the steps of the museum and headed
off toward the post office. It was a glorious fall day,
not too warm and not too cool, and the sun shone
down through golden leaves so that even the air itself
seemed to be gilded.

She strode past Windham Hall, where most of the literature classes were held, and then past Strathmore Tower for the language arts. If you climbed to the top of Strathmore and looked down, you could see that Havenport was a tiny, tree-filled quadrangle nestled between ancient sea cliffs and the waters of Long Island Sound. Its location on the Connecticut shore meant that the falls were mild and Indian summer had a tendency to last longer than in most places.

Kate kicked through the drifts of leaves that were beginning to form. A carpet of gold heaved beneath her feet and then turned into individual leaves skittering away from her dark green pumps. She followed the trajectory of one leaf, which she had kicked higher into the air than the others. As her eyes followed its golden brilliance she noticed a man who was walking about fifty feet in front of her. She recognized his tweed jacket. It was Sam. What was he doing on campus today?

He seemed to be heading for the post office, and Kate wondered what she should do. If she kept going in his direction, she'd be more than likely to catch up to him. But the thought of talking to him again was more than a little disturbing. His eyes had a way of making her feel . . . well, uneasy. Better to avoid him if she felt uncomfortable about it. But by the time she'd made her decision, it wasn't necessary. Sam hadn't gone into the post office, but instead into the campus coffee shop next door.

Kate ducked into the post office, slipped her envelope through the campus-mail slot, and then headed back outside again.

Just as she stepped through the door to the outside, she came up hard against an unyielding male chest.

She looked up and found herself staring into a pair of golden-amber eyes. Sam's eyes.

"Hello," he said with a note of surprise in his voice, and then he reached out to steady her on her feet.

Kate began to feel the familiar tremors his touch seemed to set off. She was actually quaking in front of the man! If she hadn't been so disturbed by her reaction, she might have thought it quaint. As it was, she felt considerably annoyed by her body's betrayal of her mind.

Sam's hand dropped from her arm as they stood there, blocking the entrance to the post office. A student slithered through the narrow space that separated them.

"I think we should move," Sam said. He headed indoors and Kate headed outdoors. When Sam saw they were headed in opposite directions, he reversed his route and landed on the sidewalk in front of the door, next to Kate.

"I wasn't expecting to see you again," said Kate. It was the first thing that popped into her head.

"Maybe you were really hoping you wouldn't see me again," Sam replied with a self-deprecating grin.

The man wasn't totally without humor. "Was it that bad?" she asked.

"No. I just thought it was for you." His eyes began probing into hers again. She wondered what he expected to find.

"I'm still all in one piece," she answered flippantly, and then regretted it because Sam took the opportunity to verify her remark.

He surveyed her from the tip of her green pumps, up her well-formed legs, to the slim green skirt that emphasized her softly rounded hips, and on to the wine-colored sweater that clung provocatively (or so Kate sensed) to her full breasts. When he'd completed his voyage up her body, his eyes met hers again. He didn't have to say anything. The heightened color of his eyes, where green flecks now shone, mixed with gold, spoke for him.

Kate had been looked over by men before and she'd always disliked that kind of physical assessment of a woman's worth. But that didn't seem to be what Sam was doing. There was appreciation in his eyes, not a leer, and she even sensed admiration within their depths. She found that she didn't mind him looking at her that way at all, and that was why she immediately interrupted his examination.

"I'm sorry, but I'm late for an appointment." She began to walk away. "But it was nice to see you again."

Sam headed in her direction. "Perhaps we could have lunch together?"

"No, I'm sorry. I have an appointment with Radley Davis and I can't break that."

Sam looked surprised. "I didn't think—"

Kate interrupted immediately since she knew what he was going to say. "You didn't think I had the nerve," she challenged.

He regained his assurance. "I know you have the nerve," he said.

"Well, then?" she asked.

He looked at her strangely, his face a little crumpled and askew. But then his expression assumed its usual easygoing geniality once more.

"I won't keep you," he said finally.

"Good-bye, then," Kate replied. She turned and walked back toward the museum, but thirty seconds after she had left Sam, she half turned to look back. He was still standing on the sidewalk where she'd left him, a puzzled look on his face.

Alexander Jensen was just hanging up his phone when Kate entered his office. In spite of their differences of opinion, Kate liked Jensen. A roly-poly, good-natured man in his fifties, he was one of the country's top experts in Italian quattrocento art.

"More congratulations on Helen's exhibit," he told her, gesturing toward the phone.

"Wonderful. It's a terrific show."

"I imagine I'll be hearing the same thing a month from now when your show opens, Kate." He smiled at her kindly.

"If it opens..." she responded testily.

"Now, Kate, it won't help to start the day in such a bad temper." Kate realized Jensen was teasing her because he knew she had come to his office to ask him for more funds and he was going to tell her that he didn't have them. Nevertheless, she went ahead with her pitch.

"Alex, I'll be perfectly honest and direct with you, and not waste any time beating around the bush. I need more money." She flopped down into the soft armchair in front of his desk.

"Oh, no, not this again." He grinned at her amiably, his pudgy cheeks dimpling. "I've given you the money for the loan shipping and the insurance to cover the paintings while they're here, and I've promised to have our conservator clean them and fix up the frames. I've even tossed in some extra funds for the party opening night. More than that I cannot do."

"But, Alex, you know those walls will need to be

painted. They're still green from the last show."

"It's a lovely green. So soothing, so restful." Was he egging her on or was he being maddeningly sincere?

"Like a hospital waiting room. Abstract expressionist paintings are not soothing and restful, Alex. They're bright. They're shocking. The only way they look good is against stark white. Not hospital green."

"If the paintings are good, they'll look wonderful against any color. Maybe that's your problem, not the walls." He was baiting her.

"Alex, I'm not going to get into *another* senseless argument with you about the merits of abstract expressionism. You ought to be ashamed of yourself—director of a museum and completely prejudiced against anything that's not in your field. Nine-tenths of the art of this world isn't in your field."

"A man's entitled to his prejudices," he replied equably.

Kate was glad she and Alexander Jensen had such a good working relationship, because it meant she could always say exactly what was on her mind. He was a man who enjoyed being difficult, but at least he could joke about it.

Kate had only one card and she played it while she could. "You painted Helen's walls."

"No, I didn't."

Kate looked at him in surprise. She knew he wouldn't lie to her; Alex always played fair.

"Helen had help from outside sources. You're just going to have to do the same," he said firmly.

"You mean she used the money President Simpson gave her to paint the walls?" Alex nodded, but before he could speak, Kate continued, "If you're about to suggest I ask President Davis for the money, save your breath. Didn't you see his letter in this morning's paper?" Kate said nothing about the reply she'd just mailed. It had been an impulsive gesture, and already she was beginning to regret it.

"No," Alex said, "but I spoke with him at the opening."

"So he did come by last night," Kate mused out loud.

"Did you know he was coming?" Jensen asked her sharply.

Sam's golden eyes floated across the back of her mind. "Someone told me he might. What did he say?" Kate asked.

"He's casting us off from the rest of the college for the time being. Says Havenport has to get itself back on its feet and can't do it if it's going to be burdened by organizations that should be self-supporting anyhow."

"The skinflint," Kate said heatedly.

"He doesn't have much choice. Would you rather he kept the money coming our way and the college folded? If Havenport folds, we fold, too. It's as simple as that."

Kate hadn't thought about it that way. What Alex said made sense, and yet, there was still something about the way in which Davis was going about his cost reductions that rubbed her the wrong way.

"There must be other ways of cutting the budget besides the way he's chosen," Kate offered.

"Maybe there are, but after speaking with him last night, I doubt anyone could get him to consider them. He's a strong man and he believes that what he's doing is right for the college. I tend to trust the man. He's a Havenport alumnus and his family's lived in this town for generations. I think one of his ancestors might even have founded the college. He's not in it for his own fame and fortune."

"Well, I think he's wrong," Kate said adamantly.

"Tell him that yourself. I told him the same thing last night, but I'm a fat old man, and you're a lovely young woman. He might not be completely immune to your charms." Alex's eyes twinkled.

"What are you suggesting?" Kate bristled at his implication that she could use feminine wiles to get what she wanted. Did he know what had happened in Dallas with David Atwood?

"Helen told me that she spoke with you at the opening and gave you some tips about fund-raising. What did she tell you was her most successful tactic?" Jensen looked at her closely.

"The smile." Kate bared her teeth and gave him a comical approximation of a disarming smile. It made Alex laugh.

"That's right. And you believed her, didn't you?" Jensen's voice was taking on the overtones of a schoolteacher's wheedling drone, all in jest.

"Yes," Kate answered playfully, like an obedient pupil.

"Well, then, Kate, smile, smile, smile. Smile at Davis. Smile at our trustees. You can even smile at me every once in a while."

"Yes, Alex." She felt as if he were the coach and she were the boxer being prepped for the big fight. She rose from the armchair to leave.

"Kate?" Alex said as she made her way to the door.

"Yes?"

"If all else fails, I'll scrape up the money to paint

your walls. I never liked that green: It does look like a hospital room."

Kate beamed a smile back at him.

"Wonderful," Alex encouraged her. "Wonderful. Use it on Davis. It has the true ring of sincerity."

Kate laughed. "Thanks, Alex. I knew I could count on you."

"Only if all else fails..." he warned as she headed out the door.

Kate went back to her office, feeling as if she'd just been put through a blender on Pulverize. Jensen was such an old bear of a man, but she knew he'd come through if she got desperate. He really only pretended obstinacy. But Radley Davis was a different story. Apparently, his obstinacy was the real thing.

On her desk was a phone message from Helen with the name and number of the trustee she had told Kate about last night. Beneath that was a short note from Jane saying that Helen wanted Kate to call her back and that the matter was urgent. Kate wondered what it could be about as she dialed Helen's number, but her curiosity wasn't satisfied because Helen was out to lunch. So, apparently, was Jane, although she had left the loan forms she'd been working on on her desk, completed and ready for Kate's signature.

Kate glanced at her watch: twelve-thirty. There was no time for lunch before her appointment with Radley Davis, and she wasn't really hungry anyway. Anxiety had never had a beneficial effect on her appetite.

Now that Alex had made it clear that he wasn't going to give her any more funds unless she exhausted all other avenues, the meeting with Davis became much more important. Kate found the idea of asking wealthy people for contributions slightly distasteful, but that's just what she'd have to do if Davis turned her down. If only Havenport were as well endowed as the museum she'd worked at before in Dallas. But then, that arrangement had had its problems, too . . . Kate refused to think of them now.

She had just enough time to sort through the material on the projected expenses of her show before she headed for the president's office. She grabbed the file out of her drawer and flipped through it quickly, noting that if she cut a few corners here and there, she wouldn't need a very large amount of money. If Davis would only give her half, she'd be grateful for that.

Kate rose from her desk, gathered her papers together, placed them in her briefcase, and headed out the door. It was time to meet Radley Davis face to face.

On the way to his office, she thought about the president. From what she'd heard, he wasn't very much older than her twenty-seven years, probably in his mid-thirties, which surprised her, because his letters in the paper read as if they'd been written by a crochety old fussbudget. Maybe he was the kind of man who'd always been old, who had no sense of humor, and who only saw the world in terms of dollars and cents. If that was the case, she knew she'd never be able to get through to him.

She stepped into the building that housed the president's office and walked quickly, with a bit of a nervous hitch to her stride. She'd give it her best. That was all she could do.

Kate announced herself to a secretary sitting at an old oak desk outside the president's office and then sat down, uneasily flipping through some academic journals. Finally, the secretary's intercom buzzed; she picked up her phone, listened, and then motioned for Kate to go into President Davis's office.

Here goes nothing, Kate thought to herself as she stepped through the doorway and prepared to extend her hand for a handshake. But what she saw made her hand freeze at her side. The man sitting behind the president's desk was Sam!

Chapter 3

"SAM!"

He leaped up to close the door behind her and then turned with his hand outstretched.

"Sam *Davis*," he said, emphasizing the last name.

Kate placed her hand in his only because she was replying to his gesture automatically. Sam gave it a good shake and then let it go.

"And you're Kate Burnham. But I think we've met before."

Kate looked at him as if he were out of his mind. "Sam Davis?"

"My father was Radley, too, so they called me by my middle name, Sam. It was a lot less confusing that way." He smiled at her as if it should be obvious why he was called by one name but used another.

"Wait a minute." Kate shifted her briefcase to her other hand and then rubbed her free hand against her forehead. "You're Radley Davis, but you go by the name of Sam. Does that mean you're the president here? Are you President Davis?"

"Yes," he said simply and grinned. "That's me."

"Why you . . . !" Kate almost heaved her briefcase at him but thought twice about it. She didn't want to start off the academic year with a charge of assault and battery. "Why, you're a . . ." She paused to think of a polite way to put it and then threw all caution to the wind. "You're a liar!"

"Not exactly," Sam said suavely. "Won't you sit down?"

"I don't intend to stay one minute longer. This is a farce. I can't believe the president of a college would indulge in a game like this. You're a disgrace!" Kate had never been good at restraining anger.

"You're going to have to control that loose tongue of yours, Kate. It's already gotten you into enough trouble, hasn't it?" He sat behind his desk and held his hands together in steeple formation, looking for all the world like a mobster who was about to make her an offer she couldn't refuse, except that he was smiling—indeed, grinning from ear to ear.

"You told me your name was Sam." Kate was trying to figure out what to do about the situation. She felt as if she'd just entered a strange new world that was topsy-turvy.

"It *is* Sam."

"But you led me to believe . . ." Kate began.

"You jumped to conclusions. I said I was a friend of one of the trustees, and I am. I've know Chilton Harrison for years." He was still smiling.

"You were toying with me. You'd overheard what I was saying," Kate stated, furious.

"Let's say I was just doing some informal polling about the new president's popularity and I found out what I wanted to know. You don't like him."

"I don't like *you,*" Kate said firmly, contradicting him, or rather, reaffirming what he said, or . . . Good Lord, the situation was going from bad to worse. And she was getting that horrible feeling of helplessness she used to have when she was in Dallas and David was manipulating her.

"You could have told me when we met this morning," Kate accused him.

"You were in too much of a hurry, Kate. You couldn't wait to get away from me." He looked offended.

"That's no excuse. You deliberately tricked me. It's abominable!"

"See, you don't even know me," Sam said as he leaned forward in his chair, "and you've already passed judgment. I wouldn't call that fair."

"And I wouldn't call deceiving me about your true identity playing fair, either."

"Let's say we're even, then." Sam leaned back with a satisfied smile on his face. Kate had to admit that he was adept in a battle of wits. He'd twisted things around so that instead of him being the sole culprit for deceiving her, she appeared to be equally in the wrong.

Kate was thinking fast, trying to figure out a way to maintain at least a shred of dignity in the midst of all the madness. "All right. Let's make a deal, then," she said finally.

"What?" Sam looked fascinated.

"Let's pretend none of this ever happened. Since we're even and all . . . let's pretend we're just meeting for the first time." It was ridiculously stupid, grown-up adults playing "Let's pretend," but Kate considered that to someone whose mind worked like Sam Davis's, it might make a certain amount of wacky sense.

"Agreed. Now, Miss Burnham, please take a seat."

"Thank you, President Davis." She sat in a straight-backed chair in front of his desk.

"Call me Sam. You already have," he offered.

"I thought we were pretending..."

"All right. But may I call you Kate?"

"You don't know me well enough to call me Kate."

"When will I?" His look was devilish.

Never, she wanted to say, but "I'll let you know" was what she answered.

"Fair enough." He leaned back in his chair and waved a hand at the window to his right. "Lovely weather, isn't it?"

"Delightful," Kate answered dryly.

"And you're wearing a lovely outfit."

"I don't see how that applies to the subject at hand," Kate replied, her antagonism toward Sam heating up again.

"And you have the loveliest eyes. Blue, aren't they? Or more gray? When I first met you, they reminded me of a stormy sea."

What was the man up to? Was he trying to drive her to distraction so she'd forget why she'd come to see him?

"I fail to see what that has to do with why I'm here."

"I just thought you might like to know."

"I already know what color my eyes are."

"But did you know that they looked like a storm-tossed sea? Or that when you're angry they snap and flare like fireworks?"

"This is the most unprofessional display of...of..."

But Kate couldn't think exactly what it was the most unprofessional display of. "This is unprofessional," she amended lamely.

"I just thought you might like to know," he said again, obstinately.

"You're repeating yourself."

"I'm waiting for you to ask me why I think you might like to know."

Kate felt like a laboratory rat running through the same maze over and over again and not knowing the reason why. She gave in. "Why?"

"Because when a woman's attracted to a man, she likes it when he compliments her." He sat there smugly, with a big smile on his handsome face.

Kate shot out of her seat as if she'd just been launched by a booster rocket. "This is completely out of hand! This is absolute madness!"

"When I shook your hand yesterday, I felt you tremble ever so slightly. You can't deny that, Kate," he said calmly.

"I tremble all the time. Uncontrollable muscle twitches." Kate suddenly understood that the only way to deal with Sam Davis was to start making things up, just as he'd made up his identity as the trustee's friend and just as he was making up her attraction to him. But a little voice inside Kate piped up and whispered, "You *are* attracted to him, dummy. And obviously he's attracted to you." Kate blessed her little voice; it had given her a way out of the mess. She sat back down.

"I think what you refer to is merely a matter of projection. You're attracted to me, obviously, and so you assume the feeling's mutual. It isn't." She reached down to the side of her chair and pulled her briefcase onto her lap. "Now that we've figured that out, can we please get down to business?" She began to pull folders out of her briefcase and then tapped their stiff cardboard edges against the leather of her case impatiently.

"I don't think we've figured that out yet," Sam said stubbornly.

"I don't really care—" Kate began.

"Oh?" He left his chair and came over to where she was sitting. Standing directly in front of her, he said, "But I do."

"I will not be intimidated," Kate stated with conviction. "I've come here to do business and that's exactly what I intend to do. I suggest you do the same."

He leaned down until his eyes were at the same level as hers and then he turned on his golden gaze full force. Kate had to meet it and try to stare him down. She felt herself getting weaker and weaker as she tried harder and harder to keep his amber eyes from getting to her.

"I suggest we make another deal," he whispered throatily.

"What?" Kate's voice was more like a whimper than the strong, clear bell tone she wanted it to be.

"I suggest we both agree that we're attracted to each other."

"But it's not true. I'm not attracted to you."

"The fact that it wasn't true didn't stop you from making a deal that we'd pretend we'd never met."

"That was different," she answered uneasily. His knee was brushing insistently against her own.

"Make this different, too, Kate." He leaned closer and closer, his full, ripe lips hovering dangerously close to her own.

His eyes locked with hers and Kate felt again as if she were being swallowed up by their sweet golden depths. It was the most extraordinary feeling—as if her whole body had been reduced to the size of a dust mote and she were being drawn in on a wave of golden light. She could feel the warmth of his gaze caressing the entire length of her body and enfolding her in its heat.

She closed her eyes to stop it, but when she did, his mouth touched hers softly and then more insistently as he pressed his lips against hers with a pliancy and agility that quite literally took her breath away. The kiss was exploratory and tentative at first, and then, as he began to become more assured of her response, he heightened his efforts by nipping lightly at her lips and running the tip of his tongue between their tightly pressed edges.

Kate was trying with all her strength not to respond, but his desire was too persuasive. She felt a surge of passion that she'd hardly known had existed within her. Her lips parted, and Sam's tongue delicately entered her mouth and lapped gently at its moist depths.

Involuntarily, her arms wrapped around his neck, and she felt the short hairs there prickle the soft underside of her flesh. The sensation seemed to send her off even farther than his kiss. Her blood began to rush through her veins and course like a flooding river to her ears, where it pounded like a bass drum, and then to that secret place where all desire begins and ends. Suddenly, she felt as if she were drowning in Sam's kiss, and she had to pull away from his mouth to gasp for air before she went under for good.

Her head lowered and she breathed in deeply and

rhythmically, hoping to control the beating of her heart. Sam's husky frame straightened and he stood before her in apparent triumph.

Finally she looked up at him. His expression showed a mixture of feelings. She saw the hint of a smile and a trace of his lingering excitement. Kate could only wonder what he would do next. Mechanically, in self-defense, she pulled out her folders and began riffling through the papers.

"What I wanted to speak to you about..." she started firmly.

"Oh, Kate," he said, sighing and shaking his head. "You are one in a million."

What did he mean by that? That she'd let a man kiss her and then pretend it had never happened? She felt so confused, so unnerved, that the only way to regain her equilibrium was to get back to business. "Look, Sam Davis, or Radley Davis, or whoever you think you are today, you're the one who suggested I tell the president what I thought about his new policies. So here I am." She shuffled her papers impatiently. "I want to discuss your new policy concerning the museum."

He returned to his desk and sat behind it. "If you're hoping to convince me to change my position, you may as well stop now."

"Then why did you suggest yesterday that I try to change your mind?"

He gazed at her calmly. "I never said you could change the president's mind; I merely said he'd like to hear your views."

Kate hated feeling as if she were being trifled with, and that was exactly how she felt at the moment. But in the hope of making him see reason, she tried to remain reasonable herself.

"I have an exhibition coming up and I need funds. Your *predecessor*"—she emphasized the last word pointedly—"was generous in his support. You can't just leave us high and dry," she finished ardently.

"I have no other choice. If you'd like to see why, I can show you the figures. But I wish you'd take my word for it."

"The amount I need isn't astronomical," Kate replied, pressing the point.

"All the same, you're going to have to find it elsewhere. I can't give you a penny." Now he was beginning to sound angry. "There are people who've supported the museum before, and they'll have to support it even more now."

"But we had no warning. You just sprung this on us and it's not fair. We can't survive..." She was heating up to her argument.

"The college can't survive unless costs are cut drastically, Kate," Sam said calmly. "I've made up my budget for the year and it doesn't include any funds for the museum. It's not as if I've singled out the arts. Everyone at this college has to tighten his or her belt. That's just the way it is." Kate could see from the expression on his face that he was adamant in his refusal. Alex had been right. The man was immovable.

"And you don't think that the arts are important to the students and the community of Havenport? Why do you think they're here? To learn how to cut corners?"

"I think they're here to get an education, and if

they don't follow the guidelines I've laid down, there won't be a college for them to get their education at. We'll go under. And so will the museum."

"Is that your final word?" Kate asked, even though she knew the answer.

"Yes," he responded firmly.

Kate gathered her material together and placed it back in her briefcase. "I think we have nothing more to say to each other," she said coldly, preparing to leave.

Sam's head shot up. "I think we have a lot of things to say to each other." His eyes beamed their golden rays at her again, but she evaded their grasp.

"You've said you won't give me any funds. I think that ends our discussion."

"It may end our discussion about the problems of your museum, but there are other things. . . ."

Kate rose to leave. "There is nothing else I care to discuss with you, President Davis." She turned to walk out the door.

He jumped up from behind his desk and placed himself between her and the door. "And what about our deal?"

"The only deal I remember making with you was to pretend we'd never met." Kate was avoiding even the thought of the other deal Sam had suggested— that they agree they were attracted to each other. The look on his face told her that he knew she was avoiding it, and she was surprised when he let her get away with it.

He stepped back from her. "If that's the way you want it," he said.

If she didn't get out of there soon, she'd find herself

backing down from her resistance to him. She'd vowed that she'd never mix her professional relationships with her personal ones ever again, and she had no intention of breaking her vow. Sam was attractive, she was drawn to him, and his kiss had been ... like nothing she'd ever experienced before. But he was dangerous. He made her knees feel weak and her brain numb just when she needed strong knees and a sharp mind.

Kate opened his office door and passed through. Behind her, she heard him say softly, "But you are attracted to me, Kate Burnham, and someday ..."

The door swung shut before she heard the end of his remark.

Kate headed back to the museum in a daze. She had thought she'd been put through a blender after speaking with Alex that morning; now she was fully convinced that she'd been run over by a Mack truck after her conversation with Sam Davis. The shock of seeing him behind the desk and then his kiss ... Kate pressed her fingers to her lips. They still felt warm from the heat of it. She'd never been kissed like that before. A shiver of excitement went down her spine.

She went up to her office and passed by Jane's questioning face. On top of her desk was a note written in Helen's hand, asking her to call her immediately. Kate picked up the phone and dialed. Helen herself answered.

"Kate! Oh, I'm so glad you called. There's something I have to tell you."

Suddenly it dawned on Kate what the urgency of Helen's phone calls that morning had meant. Helen was going to warn her that Sam was Radley Davis. She must have been reintroduced to him at the party after Kate had left.

"You don't need to," Kate said wearily. "I found out myself."

"That that Sam fellow was really President Davis?" Helen asked anxiously.

"Exactly. I made an appointment with Davis for one, and when I went into his office it all became clear. He was so gracious about helping me put my foot in my mouth."

"Oh, Kate, you poor thing. It wasn't very nice," Helen commiserated.

"It's water under the bridge now," Kate said, and then sighed.

"How did he react to the whole thing?" Helen asked.

"As if it were a joke. He found it amusing. I found his little games pretty shocking behavior for a president."

There was silence over the telephone, and then Helen began to speak tentatively. "I think there's more to this than just a difference of opinion between the president of Havenport and the museum's curator of American art."

"What?"

"To be blunt, Katie, I think you turn him on," Helen said, and then laughed.

"Helen, it isn't funny. The man's despicable." Kate slouched down so low in her chair that an inch or two more and she'd be on the floor. Had the whole world gone crazy?

"When you left, he kept looking over toward the coatroom as if he wanted you to come back."

"So he could make more of a monkey of me," Kate replied acidly.

"I don't think that's what he had in mind," Helen said.

"I don't care what he had in mind. I just hope I never have to see him again."

"I don't think that's very likely."

"Well, then, I'll ignore him."

"'Methinks the lady doth protest too much,'" Helen joked.

"Helen, please. I've just ruined whatever chance I had to get money from the president of Havenport, and all you're interested in is Sam Davis's romantic interests."

"He is a very attractive man, Kate, and you can't just live for your job."

"Does that mean I have to throw myself at the first available man I run into?"

"No, that's not what I meant."

"We don't even know him, Helen. Maybe he's just, well . . ." How could she put this delicately? "Maybe he's just interested in my body." There was no way to put it delicately.

Helen laughed. "But you'll never be sure unless you give yourself the chance to get to know him."

"I'm not interested in getting to know him. I'd rather forget about the whole thing. Could we change the subject?"

"All right." Helen gave up. "I gave Jane the name and number of my friend. Are you going to give him a call?"

Kate answered quickly, relieved that they were finally getting back to business. "I'll call him right now and ask him to have dinner with me tomorrow."

"Fine. And good luck," Helen said.

"Thanks," Kate said. "I'm due for some." She and Helen said their good-byes and then Kate hung up the phone.

For the rest of the afternoon she threw herself into her work. It was the only way she could keep herself from thinking about Sam Davis's lips.

Chapter 4

THE DINNER WITH Helen's friend wasn't a complete disaster, but it couldn't have been called a success, either. Robert Ludlow, or Bob, as he insisted upon being called, had hemmed and hawed through the soup, salad, and roast beef while he told Kate the story of his life, punctuated by discreet hand touchings and winks. Finally, over dessert, he told Kate that he just didn't think that "at this time" he could contribute anything to her exhibition. Kate accepted his refusal graciously, passed up his kind but suspect offer of a ride home, and wrote the whole matter off as an educational if fruitless experience.

Now, a day later, she was standing in the empty exhibition hall, looking at the green walls and trying to convince herself that the color really wouldn't be all that bad. It was a losing battle; she felt queasy just looking at them. As she remembered, the walls had been stunning with the previous show's pre-Columbian terra-cottas, but next to the bright colors of the abstract expressionist paintings they would look . . . well, *bilious* would be putting it kindly.

She had a card up her sleeve, though. There was still one more person she could ask for a donation: a dealer in New York she'd befriended while she was researching her show. She was reluctant to ask him for money because their relationship was still somewhat new, but she supposed she could hop on a train to New York the next day, visit him, and subtly reveal her problem in the hope that he'd offer to bail her out, since some of his gallery's paintings were in the show. If that proved unsuccessful, she could always dip into what little was left of her savings account. For even though Alex had said he would paint the walls for her if she couldn't find a donor, there were still other expenses to be covered, like printing up labels for each painting and running off guides to the exhibit.

She pulled out some of the paintings from the storage room and began to prop them against the walls to get a rough idea of how they would actually hang. As she worked she couldn't help but wonder how David Atwood would have handled the situation.

She sighed as she slid a small watercolor across the floor. The truth of the matter was that David Atwood never would have found himself in the predicament she was in. He was a master at fund-raising. He was also an eminent scholar, a noted expert in his field, and a charming, handsome, witty, and debonair bachelor. His appeal had been irresistible from the start.

Kate thought back to her first year at the Collier Museum in Dallas when David had taken her under his wing. She was fresh out of graduate school and still wet behind the ears. She knew nothing about museum work and hardly anything about herself and her capabilities. She had accepted his tutelage gratefully. It had made her feel so special.

But later, when she was ready to stand on her own two feet, David hadn't been willing to give up his domination of her. He still wanted to be the teacher and expected her to remain the awestruck student. Since his power at the museum had been absolute, when Kate tried to take matters into her own hands and plan her own exhibitions with her own ideas, he had vetoed the projects.

She had loved David, or at least she had thought she was in love with him, but the relationship had ended in a nasty way and left Kate with bitter feelings. At least she had learned a valuable lesson: She would never mix her professional and romantic relationships again, and she would never, ever, accept help from a man whose power could affect her career.

As Kate continued to separate and prop paintings against the walls, she forgot her thoughts about David Atwood and became more and more excited about how the show was shaping up. It really would be smashing if she could translate what was in her head into reality; that was always the hardest part of any show. She was trying to decide if she should put a small Pollock gouache next to an even smaller Rothko oil study when she heard someone enter the room. She felt a sharp tingling down her spine just before she turned to see who it was.

Sam Davis stood at the entrance to the room with his hands stuck nonchalantly into the pockets of his jacket as he looked around at the paintings and, finally, at Kate. She felt a quick jolt as their eyes met. Oh, no, she thought to herself, here we go again . . . She leaned the two paintings she had been considering against the wall, dusted off her hands with a quick, nervous gesture, and then went forward to greet him.

"Hello, Kate," he said just a trifle too heartily. "Couldn't resist stopping by to see what Havenport's most dynamic curator was up to."

"Trying not to get nauseous looking at these green walls," she joked. What was Sam Davis really doing there?

"I think it's different," he exclaimed cheerfully.

"You are too kind, President Davis," Kate replied sarcastically.

"Oh." He pondered a moment. "You mean you don't want the walls to be green?"

"Oh, brother," Kate muttered. Sam Davis had the most infuriating habit of playing the idiot just to annoy her. He'd done it during their appointment the other day, and now he was doing it again. Sincere stupidity, Kate thought, was forgivable, but presumed stupidity was not. She decided to ignore him. What could make a man feel more unwanted than to be completely ignored? She returned to her painting and left Sam standing uneasily in a corner of the room. But he didn't stay there long.

"What are you doing?" he asked as he came up behind her and stood so close that she could smell the crisp tang of his after-shave lotion. It smelled very . . . masculine.

"Looking at paintings," she replied noncommittally.

"I know that, Kate." He edged over so that he was standing right at her side and gazing into her eyes.

Again, Kate had that strange sensation of shrinking in size and being drawn into Sam's eyes. She moved away from him nervously.

She cleared her throat and said, "I'm trying to decide where to hang the paintings."

Sam picked up the small gouache she had been contemplating before he had entered. "Pollock, isn't it?"

Kate looked at him curiously. "I'm surprised you know that."

"Oh, I know a few things about art," he replied absently as he continued to look at the picture in his hand. "This is very early, isn't it?"

Again, Kate was surprised at his knowledge. "Yes, just before he began to do the action paintings. It's still slightly figurative."

He put the picture down and then picked up the oil study. "It will look very nice next to this Rothko."

Kate was intrigued. Neither of the works were signed. "How do you know these things?"

Sam leaned against the wall and crossed his arms over his chest. "Back in my younger days," he grinned, "I studied art. Even painted a bit myself."

Kate was flabbergasted. "Then why are you so against art?"

"I'm not," he said simply. "But I think there's something you need to know about me."

"I'm all ears." They stood across from each other, only inches away, and Kate found the closeness of him more than a little disconcerting.

"Actually, I'm two different people," he claimed.

What was he going to say? Kate thought to herself. That late at night he grew hair and sprouted fangs?

"Oh, please tell," she replied.

"Don't be so sarcastic, Kate," he said with a weary sigh. "I'm trying to be honest with you."

"That's a refreshing change," she snapped back. She had to keep reminding herself that he had tricked her the other day; otherwise she might start to like him too much. He had a vitality and a quickness of mind that were very engaging.

"Do you want to hear what I have to say or do you want to continue proving how obnoxious you can be?" he asked, heatedly.

Now it was Kate's turn to sigh. She didn't think it was possible for them to spend more than five minutes together without getting on each other's nerves. She supposed it wouldn't hurt to show him some minimal courtesy. "I'm sorry," she said. "Please go on."

Sam looked only slightly less disgruntled. "What I wanted to say before I was so rudely interrupted . . ."

Kate opened her mouth to refute his accusation, but Sam put his finger to his lips to shush her.

"What I wanted to say is that I have a job as the president of Havenport College and that means I have to act in a certain way. As President Radley Davis, I have to say that the college can't afford to support the museum. But as Sam Davis, I'm all for the museum."

So he was back to the Radley-Sam personality split again. How convenient for him, Kate thought. Whenever one of his personalities was challenged, he could always switch to the other and avoid a confrontation.

Sam cleared his throat but looked down at his feet before he spoke again. For the first time since she'd met him, Kate got the impression that Sam Davis was just a little unsure of himself. "What I'm trying to lead up to, Kate," he continued, "is this: Why don't you let me be the donor to your show?" He mumbled the words so low that Kate wasn't sure if she had heard him correctly.

"Did you just say that you want to be the donor to my show?"

"Yes." He looked at her, his eyes snapping like gold filings flying up from an engraver's point. "That's what I'm saying. The Sam Davis me."

Kate started to laugh for lack of anything better to do with all the emotions that were bubbling up from within her. Of all the things in the world for him to say! How could he have known that she had fled Dallas determined to avoid the kind of situation he was trying to put her in? Accept money from the president of the college's own pocket when the college itself wouldn't give it to her? It was utterly preposterous!

"And how do you think the other curators here will feel about that?" Kate asked him angrily. "Don't you think they might wonder why you were giving me the money?" Oh, she had been through all this before. It was so hideously unreal; it was David Atwood all over again.

"What reason could there be, except that as a private person I want to support your exhibition?"

"Sam, surely you're not so naive. Everyone will think there's something going on between us."

"And they'd be right," Sam said. Then, before Kate realized what was happening, he was at her side and wrapping his arms around her.

Kate tried to free herself, but his grasp was unyielding. "Sam, for goodness' sake, we're in a public place."

"I don't care." He continued to hold her close and she felt her knees weakening from the sheer male force of him. "There *is* something going on between us, and I don't care who knows."

"There isn't," Kate said boldly as she looked up

into his eyes. But it was a mistake. As soon as her eyes met his there seemed to be no reason why her lips shouldn't follow suit.

Their lips touched tentatively, and then, as if the mere touch of flesh against flesh had the power to inflame, the kiss became hotly passionate and all-encompassing. Kate began to feel her will to resist evaporating, replaced by a wildness and a desire so strong that she had to cling to Sam just to remain standing. She pressed against his hard, unyielding body and felt his heart thumping wildly against her own fluttering one.

Someone coughed behind them. Kate spun around and then nearly lost her balance. She had to grab on to Sam to keep from falling as she saw who was interrupting them. It was Alex. He looked extremely embarrassed.

"I just wanted to see how you were coming along, Kate," Alex said, looking back and forth from Kate to Sam. "But I can see you're doing just fine." He turned and walked away.

"Oh, no!" Kate turned to Sam despairingly, but he seemed much more upset about their kiss ending than about being observed by Alex. His face only showed annoyance.

"Well, I guess the cat's out of the bag now," he said with relish.

"What cat? What bag?" Kate looked at Sam and then something clicked in her head. "I think you wanted someone to see us."

"You're right. I did. If enough people see, then maybe you'll see."

"See what? That you're trying to compromise my integrity at the museum?"

"Have you ever thought, Kate, that there might be more to your life than your job at the museum?"

"No," she said, and almost added "Not now," because once she had thought there was more to her life than just her career. She had thought that she could love David and be her own person, too, but it hadn't worked out that way. The situation with Sam seemed to be falling into the same kind of pattern. He would help her, and she, in turn, would be beholden to him for her success. She'd left that kind of thing behind her in Dallas and she wasn't about to get back into it again with Sam Davis.

"You're just Kate the curator, then?" he challenged her.

"Absolutely correct," she confirmed, beginning to edge away from him.

"I don't think that's true," he said. "I think you're much more than just a curator and I think we should talk about it. Let's go out for a cup of coffee together." He touched her elbow lightly.

"That's not a good idea." Kate brushed a stray wisp of hair out of her eye to shake his hand off her arm and then fidgeted with the back of her earring. She was doing her best to ignore the intensity of Sam's golden gaze.

"Why not?" he demanded.

"I'm working. I have a job. I can't just run off." She was surprised that she had been able to think up such a reasonable excuse when inside she was turning to jelly.

"The president says you may take some time off," Sam said.

"The president doesn't have any say about the museum, remember?" Kate reminded him. "The president cast us off the other day."

Sam thought about that for a moment and then challenged her: "Would you like to go upstairs and ask Alex's permission?"

He was playing dumb again, Kate realized. It was infuriating when he used that tactic to get her to bend to his will. But since there seemed no way out of going for coffee with him, she relented.

They left the museum and headed for the local coffee shop. If they were seen, Kate reasoned, she could always say they were discussing business. And at least in a public place he wouldn't dare kiss her again. Or would he? Kate never knew what Sam was going to do; he was completely unpredictable.

Kate sat across from him in a booth and Sam ordered coffee for the two of them. He folded his hands on the table and said nothing. Their coffee came and still a word hadn't passed between them. The silence was almost soothing, Kate decided; if they weren't talking, they couldn't argue. Finally, Sam spoke.

"Tell me about yourself, Kate," he said simply.

"There's not much to tell." She stirred cream into her coffee and then toyed with the spoon.

"Where did you work before you came here?" It seemed a perfectly innocent question.

"In Dallas." Kate laid her spoon down on the table and tried to sound casual. "At the Collier Museum."

"Did you like it there?" Sam certainly was persistent.

"Yes. It was founded by a rich oil baron. We never had to worry about money."

"Sounds perfect for you." Sam drank some of his coffee and then asked pointedly, "Why did you leave?"

Kate looked up at him sharply. It was almost as if

he knew what she was trying to hide and was deliberately asking questions to make her bring it out into the open. "Personal reasons," she said shortly.

"As in man-and-woman personal reasons?"

She supposed there was no reason not to tell him the truth. "Yes."

"So you've sworn off men for the time being?"

"Yes."

"Haven't you ever heard the old expression that lightning never strikes twice?"

"I don't see how meteorological quirks have anything to do with my life," she said obstinately.

Sam laughed. "Why don't you find out?"

"All right. The next time we have a lightning storm, I'll stand in the middle of an open field and see what happens."

"That's not what I meant."

"What did you mean?"

"Have dinner with me tonight and I'll tell you."

Kate almost threw up her hands in exasperation. How could she tell him that there was no room in her life for dinners with handsome college presidents? Especially when they were trying to bribe her with money.

"I won't go out with you," was all she said.

He looked at her evenly. "I'll accept that as a compliment, then, and I won't consider it your final statement."

Had the man gone mad, or was his masculine ego unable to accept rejection? "A compliment?" she said. What could he possibly mean by that?

"Obviously you have feelings toward me, and they're of sufficient strength to make you want to run away from them." He probed her eyes with a piercing stare. What he saw must have told him that he was right, because he pushed onward. "But you can't run away from me. If it's cat and mouse you want to play, that's fine. But remember, the cat always wins." He smiled at her devilishly. He was so damn sure of himself, it was absolutely infuriating.

"And this is the exception that proves the rule." Kate stood up and began to walk out of the coffee shop, but Sam grabbed her arm before she got beyond his reach. His fingers pressed into her flesh, not enough to hurt but just enough to detain her by his side.

"This is one cat who doesn't know the meaning of the word *quit*," he warned her. She could tell by the look in his eyes that he really meant it.

"And this is one fast little mouse," she replied. Kate felt a delicious thrill of excitement run down her spine. No, her mind contradicted the little tingles, it wasn't excitement; merely annoyance at his supreme arrogance. She reached over and pried his fingers, one by one, from her arm. He watched her curiously but didn't protest.

She leaned over and whispered in his ear. "Cats can be declawed, you know."

He looked up at her and shot her a look of such golden intensity that her stomach did several flip-flops. He didn't say anything. He must have known that he didn't need to.

Chapter 5

THE TRAIN CLACKED along monotonously. Only one more stop to Havenport, Kate thought, and then I can hop in a cab, head home, and collapse in bed. It had been a long day in New York City.

In the morning she'd visited the Museum of Modern Art to view a show they had just mounted on the American luminist painters. Even though it wasn't in her particular field of American art, Kate found that sometimes looking at other periods helped her formulate new approaches to her own. Then she'd had lunch with an old college chum who was now a curator at the Metropolitan Museum of Art.

After lunch she'd gone on a tour of galleries on the Upper East Side and then down to SoHo. The gallery season was in full swing in the fall, and she spent hours looking at the artwork and chatting with the gallery owners. As a curator, Kate knew that it was terribly important to keep in close contact with the people who sold art. Even though she had practically no acquisitions budget, she still wanted to know what was up for sale. There was always the chance that she could cajole Alex into giving her some extra money, and she hated to think that she might miss something really important that would add breadth to the Havenport collection.

Finally, she visited her friend, the one she intended to ask for a donation to her show, but somehow she couldn't find the right opening in their conversation to raise the subject. If she couldn't do it gracefully, Kate didn't want to do it at all. Now she was resigned to the fact that she'd have to ask Alex to paint her walls for her.

The train pulled into the station and Kate gathered up her briefcase and her purse and disembarked. She headed over to the end of the platform where the cabbies always gathered and was about to slip into a waiting taxi when she felt a presence behind her. She turned. It was Sam.

How had he known she'd been to New York and come back on this particular train?

He was smiling, and for some silly reason she couldn't help but smile back at him. It was more from nerves than from happiness at seeing him, she told herself.

"Hi, Kate," he said cheerfully. "Would you like a ride?"

"Well...I..." Before she could even summon a reply, he had placed his hand on the small of her back and was propelling her toward his car. It was a beat-up Mercedes, so old that its back fenders were fin-shaped.

"Nice wheels," she quipped.

"Don't bite the hand that feeds, Katie. The ride's free." He opened the passenger door for her.

"But I don't want this ride," she said. Now that she was getting a grip on the situation, her defenses were rising into place. She began to sidestep him. "I'd rather take a cab." But as she looked over to the taxi stand, she discovered that it was too late. All the cabs were gone.

She sighed with frustration as she got into the Mercedes. Apparently fate was on Sam's side tonight.

He went around the front of the car with an eager lope. Kate found it difficult to understand why he wanted to ride with a woman who so obviously didn't want to ride with him. She thought it might be the moon's fault: An orange harvest moon balanced like an enormous golden coin on a clump of trees next to the station.

He got into the driver's seat, turned to her, and smiled.

"How did you know what train I was on?" Kate asked.

"I didn't, but I did know you'd gone to New York. Your assistant was flagrantly indiscreet." He grinned at her lopsidedly as he inserted the key in the ignition and started the car. It hacked and coughed as if it had a cold. "I just figured that you'd taken a train sometime after five. So, seeing as how the train takes two hours to get here from New York, at seven o'clock I came down here and waited." He put the car into reverse, backed up, and then began to head out of the station's parking lot.

"You've been waiting since seven?" Kate looked at her watch; it was eight-thirty. "Don't you have better things to do?" She hoped her question would make him feel foolish.

"Cat and mouse is a waiting game, Katie. Don't you know that?" He looked at her seriously.

Kate made no reply; she merely settled into the threadbare seat and leaned as far away from him as possible. Perhaps, if she didn't say anything, he wouldn't, either, and he'd find the situation so boring, he'd decide to leave her alone. It was a meager hope, but at the moment it was the only one she had.

"So, how did things go in New York?" Sam asked. It was a direct question, which had to be answered. So much for meager hopes, Kate thought to herself.

"Fine," she replied noncommittally.

Sam turned a corner at such an angle that Kate began to slide across the seat in his direction. She grabbed on to the door pull to keep herself on her side of the car.

"Am I safe in this vehicle?" she asked. She knew that Mercedeses were solidly built cars, but this one felt as if it were running on its reputation alone, and Sam seemed to be taking a few liberties here and there with his driving.

"Perfectly safe. I've got both hands on the wheel."

Kate looked over. There were his hands all right, strong and broad, gripping the wheel. Suddenly, she was very much aware of Sam's masculine presence in the enclosed space of the car. A shivery sensation traveled up her spine.

"Any developments on the donations front?" he asked.

Kate wished she could tell him there were, but the truth was that her last hope had just been dashed today. "No," she admitted.

"My offer still stands," he said as he swerved the car around another corner and headed down the street on which she lived. She waited until he had parked the car in front of her building until she responded.

"I can't accept it."

He switched off the ignition, turned to her, and

draped his arm across the back of the seat. "Why not?" he asked.

"The only help I need is from the president of Havenport and he refuses to give it." Kate drew her briefcase up to her chest and then crossed her arms over it as if barricading herself against him.

"We've been through this before, Kate," Sam said as he rubbed his hands impatiently against the steering wheel.

"I know, but it never seems to sink into your stubborn head that I don't want your help."

"That's some way to talk to the president of your college," he teased.

"That's the problem with you, Sam Davis. Sometimes you like to play at being the president and sometimes you like to play at just being yourself. You change roles to suit your whims." She watched as he slouched behind the steering wheel and stretched his long legs out before him. Her stomach flipped over and then settled uneasily. Funny, looking at a man's legs had never made her feel like this before.

"Why don't you invite me up to your apartment for some coffee? I went to all the trouble of giving you a ride home."

"I didn't ask you to do that. Apparently you wanted to." His deviousness infuriated her. "And besides, I don't have any coffee."

"Water would be fine," he drawled. "Don't tell me there's a drought in your apartment."

He had her there. "There isn't, but I'm still not going to ask you up." His hand had moved down from the back of the seat and was resting lightly on her shoulder. Kate could feel the warm and seductive pressure of his fingers. She wanted to bolt and run, but somehow she couldn't move.

"All right, then," he said. "We'll talk here."

"There's nothing to talk about," Kate protested as she moved over toward the door and scrunched against it. Why didn't she just pull the handle and get out? What was keeping her in the car with Sam Davis?

"I don't see why you won't accept my offer. Obviously you need the money, and I like art just as much as the next person. In fact, I love art. Especially the abstract expressionists. Let me help." It was almost a command instead of a plea.

Kate wished she could say yes, if only to end his pursuit of her, because it seemed as if he was the kind of man who would never take no for an answer. But when she thought of saying yes, the image of David Atwood flashed across her mind: David telling her he would do this for her or that for her and then controlling her so that she could never do anything for herself.

"No," she said. "And that's final." She opened the door to get out of the car, but before she could set foot on the sidewalk, Sam had reached over, grabbed her arm, and pulled her back into the car.

"Then have dinner with me tomorrow."

Kate almost groaned. Would he never let up? "No."

"Why not?" he asked stubbornly.

"I don't have to give a reason. All I have to say is no."

They were getting into another one of those crazy circular arguments again. If only she had the presence of mind to break out of it, but when she was near him it seemed to Kate as if the logical part of her brain took a vacation.

"I don't have to take no for an answer," he pressed further.

"No, you don't have to, but I'd advise that you do. I'm not going to change my mind."

"I'll just keep asking, then," he said.

"I'll keep saying no," she replied in a singsong. She almost started to laugh. She couldn't believe that two grown-up adults could act in such a childish manner.

"Why don't you just give in, Kate?" He eyed her craftily. "You'd save us both a lot of wear and tear."

He had a point there, but she wasn't about to concede it. "You'll get tired of it sooner or later. Why don't you save us both a lot of wear and tear and just give up?" she parried.

"Because..." He leaned over and pulled her across the seat in one swift, strong, and graceful movement. "...I want you."

A sharp thrill of excitement shot down Kate's backbone. His face was inches away from her own, and she could feel the warm moistness of his breath against her cheek. Again she felt a delicious sense of danger.

"And what do you intend to do with me?" she ventured. She knew she was playing with fire, but at the moment she didn't care if she got burned.

"This, for starters," he said as he pulled her sharply against him.

The strength and warmth of his arms around her lulled her into not even thinking of attempting an escape. His mouth was hot and demanding against her own. The pressure of his lips was overwhelmingly persuasive, and she found herself responding to his kiss as if it were the most natural thing in the world.

At first his lips were like a soothing balm, but then they inflamed. She opened her mouth and allowed him to explore it with his tongue. It darted in and out like a flickering flame as his hands pressed against his hard, unyielding chest. She wrapped her arms around his neck and felt the taut sinews tighten even further at her touch. They melded together as if they were molten steel, the hard muscles of his legs pressing against her soft thighs.

"Kate, why do you fight me?" he moaned as he began to run his fingers underneath her sweater.

At the touch of his flesh against her own, Kate's desire burned even hotter. She felt all her resistance crumble. For the moment, all she wanted was his mouth upon hers, his hands on her now willing body. The sharp scent of him filled her nostrils, and the taste of his warm lips was like a strange and exciting aphrodisiac. How had she ever thought that she could fight the attraction that flared between them at the merest touch or glance? Wrapped in his arms, their mingling together seemed as natural to her as falling leaves in autumn, and as inevitable as the winter snows that would follow. But what would follow this kiss she was sharing with Sam Davis?

Reluctantly, Kate pulled away. She had no business indulging herself with Sam Davis. She finally had the chance to stand on her own two feet and show the world what she could do. She couldn't jeopardize that opportunity by allowing herself to be distracted by his hot and hungry kisses.

She withdrew to her side of the car and breathed deeply and evenly to calm herself. Sam, she could tell, was scrutinizing her with his glowing amber eyes. She could feel the heat of them on her without even looking. Now, how did she get herself out of her moment of weakness without seeming like an utter fool?

"I really have to go now," she said, knowing that she was taking the cowardly way out. She grasped the door handle and pulled to release the door, but the handle came off in her hand. She stared at it, not knowing whether to laugh or cry.

"I guess you're trapped," Sam said. "Unless you want to climb through the window."

Suddenly, the absurdity of the situation struck her. She began to laugh. "Will you let me out?" she asked him.

"If that's what you want." Her laughter hadn't affected him. His face was grim.

He got out of the car and came around to her side of the door and opened it for her.

"This is some car you've got here," she joked as she got out. She couldn't help brushing against him, and as she did she felt that thrill of excitement rushing through her system again. She stood beside him on the sidewalk on quavery legs. Even if she had wanted to she wouldn't have been able to dash for the apartment door. Her body was infuriatingly traitorous.

"About that dinner tomorrow..." He seemed determined to break her resolve not to see him.

"No," Kate murmured as she headed for her building. "I'm too busy; I don't have the time." She kept her eyes down, afraid that if she looked up into his, he'd melt her resolve with one of his fiery glances.

"Curator Kate," he said sardonically, "will your books and paintings keep you warm in bed tonight?"

"No, but my electric blanket will," she retorted hotly as she edged away.

"One of these days, Kate," he called after her, "you're not going to be able to think up a snappy comeback. And then I'll—"

She whirled around and tossed her head defiantly. "What will you do?" she challenged him.

His golden glance raked her from head to toe and then returned to her flashing eyes. "I'll be waiting," he said softly.

They stood as if rooted to the spot, each unwilling to concede to the other. Finally, Sam broke the silence.

"Good night, my little mouse," he said lightly, and then walked around to the driver's side of the car and got in.

Kate watched him drive away. She had a sinking feeling in the pit of her stomach that told her he wouldn't have to wait very long.

Chapter 6

KATE WAS IN her office the next morning drawing up a wall plan for the exhibition, when the phone rang. It was Alex.

"Kate, get right up here, this instant!" he barked, and then hung up.

Kate shook her head. Alex didn't sound angry but excited. What could have happened? She ran out the door and deposited herself on a chair in front of Alex's desk in a minute flat.

Alex was beaming. "You must have a guardian angel, Kate. Look what I found on my desk this morning." He passed a bulky envelope over to her.

Kate opened it. Inside were too many hundred-dollar bills to count at a glance. A slip of paper lay on top of them with a typewritten message that said: "For the Curator's Fund, American Arts."

"Oh, my!" Kate exclaimed, and then began to count the bills.

Alex took the envelope away from her. "Don't bother to count them. I already have. It's a thousand dollars."

Kate was dumbstruck. Donations didn't usually come that way. Ordinarily, they came in checks with the donor's name prominently printed on the top.

"Doesn't it say who it's from?" she asked.

"No, apparently your patron wishes to remain anonymous." Alex looked over at her with a cagey expression on his face. "Any idea whom it might be from?"

Kate looked at Alex and tried to keep her face blank. She had a very good idea whom it was from, but she didn't want to share her suspicion with Alex. Hadn't he seen her kissing the prime suspect just the other day? That was compromising enough without adding any further evidence of her involvement with the president of Havenport College.

"No, no idea," she replied.

"Well, it looks like you've got your funds now. You can paint the walls as many times as you like, maybe even throw in a little caviar for the opening-night party." He scrutinized her. "You don't seem happy."

"Of course I am." Kate lit up her face with a smile. "I'm just wondering who could be the donor."

Alex eyed her suspiciously, but he didn't say a word. Kate wondered if he had suddenly guessed the identity of the donor but was too much of a gentleman to mention it.

"No excuses, now, Kate. I expect your exhibit to be the high point of the year. I'll deposit the money myself this morning and you can draw checks on it as soon as you like."

Kate remained in the chair, lost in her thoughts. She couldn't accept the money. She'd have to make Sam take it back.

"Kate?" Alex interrupted her thoughts.

"Yes?" she murmured absentmindedly.

"Don't just sit there. Get to work!" he reprimanded.

"Of course, Alex." She jumped up and ran out the door. She had a lot of work to do, that was certain; but first she had to pay a short visit to a certain college president.

Kate headed out of the museum at a breakneck pace, kicking up clouds of brittle leaves as she hurried down the sidewalk to the president's office.

Just who did Sam Davis think he was? And more important, just who did he think *she* was? A woman so stupid that she wouldn't know right off that he was the one who had put the thousand dollars on Alex's desk?

And then an even worse thought crossed her mind: What if Alex was lying and he hadn't found the envelope on his desk that morning? What if Sam had paid an early visit to Alex and given him the money with the condition that he not tell Kate the identity of the donor? Kate wouldn't put it past him. He seemed to enjoy playing fast and loose with her reputation. It hadn't bothered him an iota that Alex had seen him kissing her the other day. Maybe . . . but she was going too far. Alex would have told her if he had known who the donor was. He didn't play games the way Radley Sam Davis did.

She swept past Sam's secretary and threw open the door to the president's office. Sam was on the phone. Calmly, he motioned to her to sit down until he finished his call, but she remained standing. She felt more secure towering above him.

She watched him as he spoke into the receiver. His hair was tousled this morning, the chestnut locks curling over his broad forehead and up against the crisp white collar of his shirt. If only the man weren't so damn attractive, it would be much easier to tell him off. Already Kate felt as if her bones were melting, but she steeled herself against his rakish good looks. Finally he hung up the phone.

Kate jumped right in. "I want to know about that money you put on Alex's desk this morning," she accused him.

"Don't you even announce yourself?" he asked casually.

"No, not always, and don't avoid the question," she retorted.

"I don't know what you're talking about," he said with a genuine, or so it seemed, protestation of innocence.

"The thousand dollars you anonymously donated to the American Arts Curator's Fund," Kate stated.

"I still don't know what you mean," he insisted. He came around to the front of his desk and pulled out a chair for her. "Care to sit down?" he asked graciously.

"No, I don't care to sit down," Kate replied, fuming. "And stop this innocent act. You left a thousand dollars on Alex's desk this morning and I want you to take it back!"

"But I didn't leave a thousand dollars on Alex's desk this morning, so I don't see how I can take it back." He lounged against the edge of his desk and crossed his legs casually. Kate should have known that he wouldn't admit to his anonymous donation.

"All right, if you won't admit to it," she said, pulling her checkbook out of her purse, "I'll write you a check for a thousand dollars and you can cash it. Then we'll be even. I won't take handouts from you. I thought I made that clear."

She put her checkbook down on the desk and began to scribble out a check. Her hand shook as she wrote. She willed the tremors to stop as she tore the check off the pad and handed it over.

He looked at her and she could see a smile playing around the corners of his mouth. He scrutinized the check and then, slowly, with a flourish, tore it in two. Kate's mouth fell open.

"Close your mouth, Kate. You're catching flies," he said as he tossed the scraps of the check into the wastebasket.

Her jaw snapped shut and she grabbed her pen. "Never mind. I'll write you another one." She began to scribble again.

"I'll just tear it up. Because, you see, I didn't leave the money on Alex's desk. Someone else must have."

"Look, Sam, I know your devious style and I want no part of it. I won't touch a penny of your money. I have my reputation to consider and—"

"Why not consider it over dinner with me tonight?" he asked her lazily, but his bright, golden eyes gave away his eagerness. "I'm rather busy now and I don't think I could give the matter my full attention."

"Oh!" Kate yelled in frustration. She felt like pulling her hair out by the roots—or did she really want to pull out Sam's? "No!" she said firmly.

"It's only fair, when you accuse someone of something, to let them explain themselves. Or don't you play fair?" he inquired.

"I play fair," she insisted before she realized that she had just consented, more or less, to dinner with him that evening.

"Good. I'll pick you up at your apartment at seven." He turned back to his desk and began to shuffle through some papers as if the matter were closed.

"I won't be there," Kate told him.

"Oh, I think you will be," he answered, and then looked up at her. "One doesn't go around hurling wild accusations at the president and expect to just walk away scot-free."

He had the most infuriating habit of changing roles whenever it suited his purpose, and she was powerless to fight him when he did.

Kate didn't say a word. She gave him the most withering glance she was capable of and then stormed out the door. She heard him chuckling under his breath as she left. He had bested her again, but this time, she vowed, would be the last.

At quarter to seven Kate was pacing back and forth across her living-room floor. She was of half a mind to dash out before Sam Davis showed up to take her to dinner. It was just what she had intended to do until she had talked to Helen Drummond that afternoon.

"Why don't you have dinner with him?" Helen had asked while they sat having coffee in one of the empty conference rooms on the ground floor of the museum.

"Because I don't want to," Kate almost wailed.

"You can't just accuse the man of something and then not give him a chance to defend himself," Helen reasoned.

"But it's more than that. Don't you see? He wants to have an affair with me!"

Helen raised her eyebrows. "I never thought I'd hear a woman griping about a man as attractive as Sam Davis pursuing her."

"You know what I mean," Kate replied. In the

short time she'd been at Havenport, she had confided in Helen the reason why she had left Dallas. The older woman had been sympathetic and had urged Kate to put the bitter experience behind her and not brood about it.

"I know," Helen said. "You think he's trying to undermine your efforts to establish yourself as a curator. You think he's trying to control you the way David Atwood did. But I don't think that's true. In fact, I think it's just the opposite."

"What?" Kate exclaimed.

"I think he wants you to succeed, that's why he offered to be your donor. I think he cares about you and wants to help you with the show."

"So he slips a thousand dollars onto Alex's desk anonymously? That's devious," Kate stated firmly.

"We don't even know if he did it, and frankly I don't think he did. He's pretty up-front about what he thinks and what he does. Someone else must have given Alex that money."

"But it's so obvious—" Kate began.

Helen interrupted her. "Only to you. To me, it isn't. At any rate, a man is presumed innocent until he's proven guilty."

Reluctantly, Kate had to agree with her. "Well, how do I get my proof? Ask for a bank statement?"

"Use your instincts. If he tells you he didn't give Alex the money, then believe him. And," Helen continued, eyeing her cagily, "if your instincts tell you to get involved with him, then go ahead."

"My instincts tell me to stay away," Kate grumbled.

"No, your fear tells you to stay away. I can already tell by the look in your eye when you say his name that your instincts are definitely pushing you toward him."

"There's no room in my life for him," Kate argued. She had enough on her mind without considering a romantic liaison with a man as unpredictable as Sam Davis.

"So make room. All work and no play..."

"...makes me a successful curator." Kate finished Helen's sentence for her.

Helen shook her head. "On the contrary: It makes you a very lonely woman. Do you really want to be one of those tough career women who live only for their jobs? That sounds like where you're heading."

Was that where she was heading? Kate shot Helen a questioning look.

"Stop being such an academic. Take a chance. Think with your heart."

Kate knew she had a heart. Hadn't it been broken before? But how did she think with it? It seemed to her that her heart didn't think at all; it merely attached itself to unsuitable males. "I don't know how to do that," she said.

"You'll learn," Helen said comfortingly, and patted her hand. "But you've got to give it a chance."

That had ended their conversation. Kate was left to ponder, for the rest of the afternoon, what Helen had said.

Since Kate had come to Havenport, there had been times when she had been excruciatingly lonely. Her eager response to Sam's kisses and the way her body craved his touch was enough proof of that. So far she had been able to escape from her loneliness with her work. But now, with Sam Davis on the scene, the emptiness of her personal life seemed to stand out in stark relief.

Kate had to admit to herself that she was tempted to become Sam Davis's lover. Kate blushed to herself. That was what this was all about, wasn't it? It was the simple attraction of a man to a woman and a woman to a man. Was Helen right? Should she take a chance?

Before she could arrive at an answer to her question, the doorbell rang. Sam himself was there, and there was no more time for idle speculation.

She opened the door and found him lounging on the doorstep, a bouquet of chrysanthemums in his hand. They were the deep-maroon ones that she loved the best. Blast his gallantry, and his unerring instincts about her. It was hard enough to resist his overwhelming sexual appeal, but when the man shared her enthusiasm for Pollock and Rothko *and* brought her a bouquet of her favorite flowers...

She asked him to come in, and he presented the flowers to her with an almost courtly gesture.

"Thank you," she said, accepting them with a smile as she motioned him to the couch. "Please have a seat while I go put these in a vase."

Settling his husky frame onto her plain, square sofa, he returned her smile. "You know, that's the first friendly smile you've ever given me. Perhaps I should send bouquets daily."

"Don't you dare," she warned, but she smiled again and watched benevolently as he stretched his legs out before him. He was wearing his usual outfit—a pair of conservative gray trousers and a tweed jacket with a button-down-collar shirt. He looked unpretentious

and open . . . and very, very appealing. Kate knew that
if she had been able to look at Sam Davis with completely unprejudiced eyes, she would like what she
saw. She sighed and purposefully marched toward the
kitchen.

A few minutes later, she returned to the living room
with the vase of flowers and set it down on the coffee
table.

"They're really lovely," she said, gazing at the
chrysanthemums.

"And so are you," he replied with evident appreciation in his voice.

Kate looked down at what she was wearing. She
hadn't bothered to change after work, knowing that
her simple navy pleated skirt and striped silk blouse
would be appropriate for wherever they decided to
have dinner.

"Thanks," she said, sitting down in a chair opposite
him.

"This is a very nice apartment," Sam said, looking
around him. "You collect things, don't you?" His eyes
had taken in the objects that were scattered about the
room. "From the fifties?"

Kate nodded her head. Again she was surprised at
his knowledge of art. "I used to go to a lot of tag
sales and thrift stores. You could always get things
from the fifties for practically nothing. Good things,
too. Up until a few years ago no one wanted them."

"And the furniture?" he asked.

"Same place," she replied. She loved the few pieces
she had. They were spare and colorful. They filled
up a room without making any kind of obvious statement, and their clean lines and simple upholstery made
them easy to take care of.

"Straightforward," he said, referring, she knew, to their conversation on the first night they had met. "Just like you."

He sent his eyes down upon her with a look that was warm and would have put her at her ease if she hadn't detected the glimmering of gold that shone in its depths. She had better be on her guard tonight. She didn't think that Sam Davis was going to play fair.

"Well, which one are you tonight, Sam or Radley?" she asked. It was probably a good idea to get that clarified right away.

"Which one would you like me to be?" he asked.

"I didn't know I had a choice," she returned, almost enjoying their banter.

"May I make a suggestion?"

Kate nodded her head.

"Let me be Sam. I think you like him better." He smiled.

Kate almost smiled back, and then caught herself. The last thing she wanted to do was encourage him.

"Okay, Sam." There seemed to be nothing else to say.

"I think it's time we went to dinner." He rose from the couch and stretched his long, powerful legs.

Kate picked up her purse and they went down to Sam's car. As he opened the door and helped her into the Mercedes, she noticed that the inside door handle had been reattached.

Sam slid into the driver's seat. "Don't worry, I fixed the handle. You can bail out at any time."

Kate didn't say anything, just shot him a glance that she hoped was withering and then settled back into the seat and let Sam drive in peace.

She rolled down her window to let in some of the crisp fall air. It was a glorious autumn evening. The sun was just setting and the sky seemed to be filled with a golden haze, but the breeze held a nip of coolness in it. Until she moved to Havenport, she hadn't known why New Englanders tended to wax so poetic about their falls. Now she knew.

"I thought we'd go to this small Italian place I like," Sam said as he drove the car toward a section of town that was even older than that in which the college stood. "Any objections?"

Kate shook her head no. Now that she was in the car with him, she was having that same sense of uneasiness—or perhaps it was more wariness—that she had felt in his company before. He didn't have to say a word, or even look at her with his golden eyes, because his mere proximity seemed to set something off in her. It was hard to determine whether the sensation was sharply pleasant or painfully annoying, but it was certainly intense.

"I thought you might appreciate a less public place," he said as he pulled into a tiny parking lot next to an even smaller building.

"That was thoughtful of you," Kate replied, slightly surprised. It was his first concession to her desire to keep their relationship—if it could be called that— low-key. She began to feel a bit more relaxed.

The restaurant was an old family-run place in Havenport's Little Italy. The lighting was low and subdued and the tables were small and covered with white linen cloths instead of the ubiquitous red checks that were featured in most Italian restaurants. Fresh flowers in crystal vases sat in the middle of each table.

The headwaiter, who greeted Sam by name, led

them to a table in a secluded corner. They ordered cocktails—or rather, Sam ordered Campari and sodas for the two of them, assuring Kate that once she got past the slight bitterness of the drink, she'd soon become addicted to it. He was right. At first it tasted like cough syrup, but then the bitterness mellowed. They ordered their dinner and then, with no menus to distract them, fell into an uneasy silence. Sam was the one to break it.

"About that donation on Alex's desk this morning..." he began.

Kate waved her hand. "Forget about it. You're no longer under suspicion." Helen must have convinced her that Sam was innocent. Either that or she was just tired of arguing with him about it.

Sam looked surprised. "You mean you're letting me off the hook?" He sipped his Campari and observed her quizzically. Obviously he hadn't expected her to be so agreeable.

Kate toyed with the condensation on the surface of her cocktail glass, drawing free-form shapes with her index finger. "I figure that anyone who drives a car like yours probably doesn't have a thousand dollars to spare." She took a hearty sip of her drink and liked the way the liquid slid down her throat and made her stomach feel warm and settled, as if the Campari were drowning the butterflies that had fluttered there all day long. "And besides, even if you did leave the money on Alex's desk, I doubt you'd admit to it." She put the glass down on the table. "It's your conscience, not mine."

"I guess that's the sensible way of seeing things," Sam said grudgingly.

Kate had thought he'd be pleased that she wasn't

still accusing him of being the anonymous donor, but the look on his face seemed regretful. "You mean you want me to keep accusing you of it?" she asked.

He laughed. "The truth is, Kate, I've gotten rather accustomed to your animosity toward me. I don't know how to feel about the new, reasonable you." His golden eyes baited her.

"Do you find it boring?" she asked. Perhaps if he did she wouldn't have to worry about getting involved with him. Maybe he liked only women who were argumentative. Maybe they challenged his masculine ego or something, and without the challenge he lost interest.

"Oh, no. On the contrary, I find it very interesting. It's a whole new side of you I haven't seen before." His smile was slow and lazy and charming as he flashed her a look that burned like autumn leaves crackling in a smoky bonfire. "It makes you more . . ." He paused, either to choose the right word or for emphasis. ". . . lovable."

Kate looked at him with wide-open eyes and he looked right back at her, unabashed. Luckily their meal arrived and, for the moment, conversation became less important than sampling their dinners. But Sam wasn't about to let the issue rest.

"Does the mention of love offend you?" he asked, lifting another forkful of manicotti to his lips. He was baiting her again.

She took up the challenge. "No, it doesn't. I just don't have much use for it," she replied as she twirled linguine with clam sauce around her fork.

What she said seemed to annoy him. He put down his fork and leaned toward her. "Everyone needs love," he stated firmly. "Even curators."

"Not this curator. I'm too busy. I have an exhibition coming up and I don't have the time—"

He interrupted her. "You should make the time, Kate," he said obstinately.

Hadn't she heard that before? Yes, it was just what Helen had told her that afternoon. There seemed to be a conspiracy brewing to get her into Sam Davis's arms. Kate didn't like feeling as if she had no control over what happened in her life. She fought back.

"That's my decision," she said briskly. "I've gotten used to making up my own mind and I prefer it that way."

"Sometimes you have no choice, Kate. Sometimes love takes you unawares. Like when I saw you the first time at the museum."

Was he telling her that he was falling in love with her? The thought of it was more appealing than she would have liked. She decided to set the record straight right away.

"Physical attraction is quite a different matter from love." She hated the way she sounded, like an old-maid aunt explaining the facts of life to her teenage niece. And why was she admitting that there was a physical attraction between the two of them? Well, why not admit it? Clearly it was there, pulsating in the air whenever they were together. But it had nothing to do with love.

"Well, at least you're admitting that you're attracted to me. That's a beginning," he said.

"Beginning and end," she stated. She picked up another forkful of linguine and drew it to her lips, but suddenly she wasn't hungry anymore. She put her laden fork back down, picked up her napkin, patted her lips, and rose from the chair. "I've lost my appetite. Would you mind if we left?" She knew it was useless to ask, but she asked anyway.

"Yes, I'd mind. I'd mind very much. Please sit back down; there's something I want to tell you."

Kate reseated herself. If she let him have his say, then maybe he'd take her home and their silly charade would be over that much sooner.

"Kate," he said seriously, "you're confused."

She looked at him, agape. *She* was confused? "Aren't you the one who can't decide from one moment to the next whether you're Sam or Radley?"

"I always know which one I am. You're the one who can't tell."

"Why don't you have name tags made up and wear whichever one you are, whenever you're whichever. Then maybe I wouldn't be so confused." The conversation was taking on that wacky circularity again. Kate knew it could only get worse.

"We're getting off the point here," he said, tapping the table with the tines of his fork.

"What is the point?" Kate demanded.

"I want to know why you've sworn off men. That is what you've done, isn't it?" His eyes were bright gold buttons, hard and round and glittering.

"More or less," she responded evasively. Why wouldn't he just leave her alone? Most men would when they understood that a woman just wasn't interested.

"But all men aren't alike. You act as if we're all the same." His eyes lighted on her plate. "Like clams."

That was an interesting analogy, and one she'd never heard before. "Maybe I don't like clams."

"Maybe you just got a bad clam." Sam smiled.

Kate had to admit to herself that comparing men

to mollusks was kind of funny, but her tentative smile faded as she thought of the distinctly unclamlike David Atwood.

"Why don't you tell me about him?" Sam asked. "Maybe it would help to talk about it."

"I don't need help," she protested, thinking that what she really needed was to get away from him, pronto. The conversation had taken a distinctly uncomfortable turn.

"But you do. You can't go on refusing to deal with one half of the human race. It's not healthy."

"It's not one half of the human race. It's you, Sam Davis. If you weren't so dense—" But before she could continue, he interrupted her.

"If *you* weren't so dense," he said ardently, over the table, "you'd stop this silly game you're playing with me and let yourself get to know me better."

"Has it ever occurred to you that I don't want to get to know you better?"

"No, it hasn't," he said. "Because all the evidence points to the contrary."

"What evidence?" Her temper was beginning to flare. He was trapping her and she didn't like it one bit.

"The way you act when you're in my arms. The way you return my kisses in that fiery manner of yours. The way your eyes dart around when I look at you. The way—"

"That's enough!" Kate exclaimed. "You're making all this up!" But she knew he wasn't. And from the look on his face, she knew that he knew she knew.

Perhaps Sam realized that he had gone too far with his last statement, or perhaps he thought that it was better just to let the matter drop for the time being.

In any case, Kate was relieved when he didn't answer her, and even more relieved when the waiter came to clear the table.

"Coffee?" Sam asked, raising his eyebrow.

Kate nodded in assent. Perhaps coffee would clear her head, which was feeling a bit woozy after the apéritif and the wine they had drunk with dinner.

When it came, the coffee was strong and fresh and brisk to taste. They sipped in silence.

Sam paid the check and complimented the head-waiter on the delicious meal, and then they left. Even on their way back to Kate's apartment they were quiet. The silence, Kate mused to herself, was so thick, it could be cut by the proverbial knife.

Sam pulled the car up to the curb in front of her building. "Good night, Kate," he said.

This wasn't what she had been expecting. The look on her face must have betrayed her feelings.

"You're wondering why I'm just saying good night, aren't you?" he asked her.

She nodded. It wasn't like him to give up like this.

"I don't know what happened to you in Dallas, but until you do decide to tell me, there's not much use in our seeing each other. You see"—he leaned over and placed his hand on hers, and this time his touch was comforting, rather than electrical—"I care about you. I can't change what happened there, but if you'll let me, I can show you that it doesn't necessarily have to happen again."

Kate remained silent. She was filled with too many conflicting emotions to say anything. Half of her wanted to tell Sam what had happened and the other half was scared.

"Kate, please. It might make you feel better to talk

about it," Sam coaxed. His hand was warm and strong around her own. Perhaps it gave her courage, or maybe she was just tired of fighting the feelings she was beginning to have for him.

She took the plunge. "Would you like to come up for a nightcap?"

Chapter 7

SAM SAT ON the couch while Kate poured two snifters of brandy. One of them was fuller than the other; that one was hers. She handed Sam his glass and then sat down in a chair opposite him. His face was expectant, but calm. She gulped some brandy, opened her mouth, closed it, opened it again, changed her mind, and then sat there in silence.

She expected Sam to say something, but he remained silent, too. Obviously, he was waiting for her to speak. But what was she going to say? She stared down into the amber liquid, trying to latch on to at least one of the thoughts that were skittering through her mind, but they evaded her. And then, to her intense embarrassment, tears welled up in her eyes and one began to slide down her cheek.

What could she say to him? How could she explain that ever since she had left Dallas and David Atwood, there had been a cold, hard shell around her heart, and now that it was beginning to crack, she felt vulnerable and afraid?

She looked over at Sam again. He was leaning forward in his chair with a concerned expression on his face, and it suddenly hit her that he, unlike David

Atwood, might be a man she could trust. She finally began to talk.

"In Dallas, I fell in love for the first time in my life."

"Was he another curator?" Sam asked.

"No, he was the director of the museum. He taught me everything he knew, and I relied on him to help me."

"That's not so unusual. Most people have a mentor along the way."

"But he was more than that." She paused. "He was also my lover."

Sam looked at her quizzically. "Should it matter to me that you were intimate with another man? Is that what bothers you?"

"No, that's not it." She shifted nervously in her chair and plucked at the upholstery. "You see, at first I needed David to help me. But then, the more he helped, the more helpless I felt. And then people at the museum began to talk about us. They said that the only reason I was successful was because of David, that I was just his puppet or tool or whatever." She was looking down into her lap now, not sure of what she could say next. It still confused her.

"Did you talk to him about it?" Sam asked.

"Yes, but he just laughed. He said that if I gave him preferential treatment—and that was just how he put it—then it was only fair that he give me preferential treatment."

Sam frowned, but didn't say anything.

"I decided that the only way I could stop the feeling of helplessness was to stop turning to David for help with my work at the museum. And so that's what I did. But David didn't like that."

"He wanted to keep pulling the strings," Sam suggested.

Kate looked up at him, puzzled. She had never thought of it that way before. "He kept putting stones in my path. Whenever I made a decision on my own, he'd veto it, or make fun of it, or tell me it was a bad decision. I loved him so much that I didn't know what to do. If I let him call the shots, I'd keep his love but I'd lose myself; and if I called the shots, I'd have my integrity but I wouldn't have David."

"What did you decide to do?" Sam asked.

"I didn't have to decide," Kate said with a bitter tone to her voice. "David decided for me. A new junior curator came to the museum. One day I went up to David's office to talk to him and walked in without knocking as I always did. There he was, kissing the new curator."

Sam got to his feet and then came over to her chair and knelt beside it while he took her hand. "That must have been awful for you."

"But that wasn't the worst part." She held on to his hand and continued, "I had an exhibition to do shortly after that. I tried to do it all on my own and it was a horrible flop. Everything went wrong and David refused to help. And then, when it was all over, he called me up to his office and gave me a long lecture, telling me step by step how I'd gone wrong. And then..." Kate wanted to go on but her throat was so tight with suppressed sobs that she felt as if she were being strangled.

"I can wait," Sam said. "Drink some brandy."

He gave her the snifter and watched as she took a small sip. The warmth of it relaxed her throat enough for her to go on.

"He said that I would never be able to do anything on my own, that I was the kind of woman who needed a man to tell her what to do. 'You'll never make it without me, Kate,' he told me. And then he said I had to leave the museum." Tears were falling freely down her face now. She wiped them away slowly, feeling the hot flush of her cheeks beneath the wetness.

"He could do that?" Sam asked.

"Yes. He had absolute power there. It took me months to find a new job. All the while I was looking for one, I had to watch David giving someone else his own special kind of preferential treatment, wondering if what he had said was true and thinking that I'd ruined my life."

"But you're here now. And you're doing fine," Sam said sincerely.

"Because I learned a lesson," Kate said. Sam was so close to her that she could smell his special scent, and his hand was strong and warm around her own.

"What was that?" he murmured as he brushed his mouth against the back of her hand. A fire began to grow deep inside her.

"That my career is more important to me than anything else. And that I'll never, ever again get involved with a man who might threaten it." She was fighting the fire with words, but words were only weightless, ephemeral things, and the flames spreading through her body were very real.

Sam rocked back on his heels and dropped her hand as if she had pushed him away. "And that includes me, I suppose." His eyes were hard and bright and challenging.

"You offered me that money so that I would be

grateful, didn't you? As well as . . . well . . ." She fumbled, not knowing how to complete her thought.

"Preferential treatment?" Sam said.

"Yes," she replied, her eyes meeting his gravely.

Sam fell back onto the floor, chuckling. Kate didn't know what to think. And then he spoke.

"I was so damn glad that you kept refusing it, because I really didn't know how I was going to be able to round it up if you said yes."

Kate's mind spun in confusion. "But then why did you offer it?"

Sam sighed, crossed his legs, and put his elbows up on his thighs so that he could rest his chin on his hands. "Because a beautiful woman was telling me in no uncertain terms that I was a nincompoop, and it suddenly occurred to me that she might be right. But as the president of the college, I couldn't go back on what I'd said, and I couldn't play favorites by exempting the museum. As a private citizen, though"—he smiled—"I thought I could make amends with my own personal offering. Because you're right: Art is terribly important."

Kate looked at him warily. "It had nothing to do with preferential treatment?"

He laughed again. "No, it didn't. What it had to do with, my lovely curator Kate, was my feeling like a fool."

She joined in his laughter, thinking suddenly what a terrific man he was, with his head thrown back and his mouth wide open with the most wonderful throaty chuckle coming out of it. He wasn't afraid to tell her that he had felt like a fool. He wasn't afraid of honesty or real feelings. He was a man she could trust.

But before she could think any more about it, Sam

was in front of her, pulling her out of the chair and into his arms.

"Oh, Kate, we've been working at cross-purposes," he said as he drew her face close to his. A tiny pulse beat throbbed at his temple, so like the pounding she felt in her own veins.

"I guess we have," she said shyly, not knowing what to do with all the feelings that were welling up within her.

"Let's make a deal," he whispered softly in her ear as his lips nibbled at the tender lobe beneath it.

Kate didn't know if she was capable of doing anything that rational at the moment. His own ear was dangerously close to her mouth, and she longed to return his tender caress in kind.

"Let's call a truce, Katie. Let's be partners, or coconspirators, or whatever you want to call it. Let's try to get along."

She felt feverish. His lips had left her ear and were trailing down the side of her neck, licking and nibbling and leaving fiery imprints behind. "What does it involve?" she barely managed to say.

He pulled away from her for a few seconds, only enough time for her to see the devilish gleam in his eyes. "Something along these lines," he said as he pressed his lips against hers and started to kiss her.

Enfolded in Sam's masterful arms, Kate felt deliciously, supremely alive. She wrapped her own arms around his neck and let her lips find the secret pleasures of his. They were soft and still held the lingering taste of brandy. She parted her lips to his and let his tongue dart between them and play inside, loving the pebbly texture of it against the smooth inner cavern of her mouth. She opened her eyes and saw his chestnut eyelashes tremble. Then his eyes opened and she could see the amber flames within.

"Is it a deal?" he asked her.

She pulled away from him. There were only a few inches of space between them, but it seemed like an enormous gap, now that she knew what it was like to be wrapped in his embrace.

"But there's still something I don't know," she said.

"What's that?" Sam asked.

Kate could tell that he was exercising an enormous amount of restraint to keep himself from pulling her back into his arms. But he must have known that she had doubts that had to be put to rest before she could go any further.

"I don't know if David is right. Maybe I am the kind of woman who needs a man to tell her what to do. Maybe I am weak and helpless."

Sam smiled. "There's not a helpless bone in your body, Kate Burnham. I can personally attest to that."

"But why would David say I was if it wasn't true?"

"Maybe David was intimidated by how strong you were, and so he tried to convince you that you weren't. People do that sometimes when they're not happy with themselves."

"But I have to prove that he's wrong," Kate said, "before I'm sure myself."

Sam looked at her, as if weighing what she said before he spoke. "You left Dallas over a year ago, but you act as if you're still there. What does it matter what David thought? Whatever you do has to be for you, not to prove that he was wrong. You've been running away from something. Why not try running toward something instead? Something that you want."

"Like you?" Kate blurted it out before she had the chance to catch herself.

Sam smiled, and the brightness of it, and the love it seemed to promise, tore at Kate's heart. "Like me," he said.

She stepped forward and allowed him to draw her into his embrace.

"But I feel so helpless when you look at me," she protested. "Isn't that bad?"

Sam sighed, and the breath from it ruffled the hairs on top of her head. It was the most intimate of gestures. "Oh, Kate, I feel the same way," he whispered.

She drew back and looked up into his eyes. They were like overflowing golden goblets. "You do?" She couldn't imagine Sam Davis feeling helpless about anything.

"Of course I do." His hand stroked her hair tenderly. "It's scary to give your heart to someone, but you can't stop yourself from doing it. You can only hope that they'll cherish your love as much as you cherish theirs."

Kate thought about that for a minute. "Are we falling in love?" she asked softly.

Sam didn't say a word, but he laughed, a delighted, loving laugh, and then pulled her closer. "I think we are, Katie. I definitely think we are."

They embraced for what seemed like hours, and then gently Sam took her hand and began to lead her down the hallway. He turned to her once with a questioning glance, wordlessly asking if this was what she wanted, and she merely nodded. She wanted it more than anything else in the world.

When they reached her bedroom, Sam sat down next to her on the bed. His eyes held hers in a glance that was liquid and golden. She let herself be drawn in, feeling weightless and pure, like swirling fog flowing through deep green valleys, or like sunlight glinting off calm, fathomless pools, turning their water into sheets of pure, shimmering gold. She felt herself falling, wondering if she would fall forever until she realized that Sam was only pulling her down onto the bed with him.

His hands began to unbutton her blouse and ironically she shivered at the heat of his touch. When the buttons were all unfastened, he pushed her blouse aside and then deftly released the clasp that held her bra together. Tenderly he lifted her breasts out of their lacy coverings and lovingly took one taut nipple in his mouth and teased it with his tongue.

The sensation was like no other she had ever felt. Sharp pinpricks of desire began to flow through her veins, or was it more like flames roaring through her bloodstream? She moaned as he undid her skirt and pulled it down over her hips.

Eagerly, she began to unbutton his shirt, and when it was free she touched his chest with the soft pads of her fingers, surprised at the silky feel of the hairs there. The tension between them was building to a fever pitch. Quickly, Sam pulled off her hose and panties. She could see his eyes widen at the sight of her naked body lying beneath him, and the sound of his sharp intake of breath goaded her desire even further. With a quick snap and pull she undid his trousers and found, to her surprise, that he was nude beneath them. Her eyes rose to his questioningly. Had he been anticipating that they would make love tonight and worn as little as possible?

He chuckled, the sound a rich, throaty burr. "Never

wear 'em," he said as he threw his slacks onto the floor. Now they were both completely naked.

He pressed his full length against her and she felt the exquisite touch of his flesh against her own. Beneath the skin of his thighs she could feel the hard musculature, and as he pulled her even closer she marveled at how wonderfully they fit against her own soft thighs. Their bodies were like the final missing pieces of a puzzle, fitting together elegantly and perfectly. Kate longed for the ultimate joining and shivered in anticipation.

She grasped his shoulders, relishing the sinews, which were as strong and willful and demanding as his mouth upon hers. His hands dipped below her waist and insinuated themselves into the place between her thighs, where he caressed the tender thorn that excited her desire even further. Shyly she reached for him, for the masculine hardness that promised her pleasure, and began to stroke him tentatively at first, and then boldly when she heard the moans erupting from his throat.

She was moaning, too, and then sighing as his hands brought her to the peak of passion and then stopped just before she went over. She knew instinctively that his teasing would bring only greater fulfillment when he finally decided to let her go. It was as though they were indulging in a splendid game, playing with one another's body like musicians searching for the perfect chord.

She teased him back, inflaming and then soothing him, until finally he could stand it no longer. He nudged her knees open with his own and then entered her, but gently, almost shyly, moving slowly and then increasing the rate of his rhythmic thrusts until she was almost delirious from the sensation. She had never dreamed that anything could feel so thrilling, so wondrous.

And then he placed his hands on either side of her face and pulled his own away from hers. His eyes burned like autumn bonfires, and her own shone back at him, sapphire-bright; bold saucy jewels in the flicker of his amber gaze.

"I knew it would be like this. I knew it would be perfect," he murmured, and then his eyes closed. She closed her own and felt herself being carried away by the ecstasy of having him inside her. She was going over the peak and he was taking her with him, down the sweet slopes of desire.

Later, leaning on his elbow, he continued to caress her, running his broad hand down the soft contours of her stomach and tickling her impishly.

"Did you know it would be like this, Kate?" he asked her. His eyes still glowed, but they were banked fires, tamed and satisfied.

"No," she responded shyly. Now that the heat of their coupling had passed, she was in a state of wonderment. She could hardly believe that it had happened. It was so extraordinarily unlike anything else she had ever experienced. "But I'd hoped," she whispered.

"Now you see"—he continued to explore her body with his hands—"that we were meant to be like this. I knew it from the start. But you, unfortunately, took a damn good bit of convincing."

He was so perturbed that she had to laugh. "Was it worth it?" she teased.

"Yes," he said fiercely, and drew her up against him. "And I intend to go on convincing you until you never have another doubt in your mind." His hands did as his words had said, and again they brought each other to the peak of fulfillment and slid down together, enraptured.

Chapter 8

KATE OPENED ONE EYE. The bedside clock indicated that it was six o'clock. In her usual foggy morning daze Kate wondered why she had woken up at six when she always awoke at eight. And then she felt the slight movement of a body next to her. So last night hadn't been a dream! Sam lay on his back, still asleep next to her, one arm across his blanket-covered chest and the other, wrist up, across his forehead. His chest rose and fell in a steady, deep rhythm, and his face was relaxed. He looked content.

She brushed her hair out of her eyes, leaned on her elbow, facing him, and wondered if she could spend the whole day just looking at him; it certainly seemed, at the moment, the most pleasurable activity on earth. But even if she decided to stay in bed all day, she doubted that Sam would stay asleep just to indulge her. She imagined that once he awoke he would be raring to get on with the day.

But until that happened, Kate was content to lie there and stare at the sleeping Sam Davis as images of their night of lovemaking flitted through her mind. His eyes burned above her as he whispered her name, and her stomach gave a quick lurch. His hands caressed her breasts and toyed wickedly with her love-swollen nipples and her heart leaped into her throat and pounded wildly. She was just about to consider the effect the memory of one of his hot kisses might produce when she saw his eyelashes tremble and then open over hazy golden eyes. He looked at her, a broad smile lighting up his face.

"You're even more beautiful in the morning than I had imagined," he said as he ran his hand through his tousled chestnut hair.

Kate lowered her head and shook it, partly to scoff at what he was saying and partly to hide the smile that she couldn't stop from spreading across her face.

Sam reached over and encircled her wrist with his fingers and then slid his hand up so that it was pressed against her palm with the back of it resting against her slightly flushed cheek. "It's true. You're lovely in the morning."

Kate laughed. "I've seen myself in the morning, Sam Davis, more times than you have, and mascara-smudged eyes are not my idea of loveliness."

He grasped her hand tightly in his and then pulled her over to his side of the bed, fitting her body closely next to him. The long, hard length of him seemed to stimulate every erogenous zone of her body. "Mascara smudges or not, you're beautiful in the morning and that's that." He wrapped his arms around her and nuzzled her hair with his nose. "You even smell good."

"You smell good too," Kate said shyly. She didn't know what to say except echo his words.

"You must have a very kinky nose, then." He laughed. "What do you say to a shower together and then some breakfast?"

She'd been right—Sam did wake up raring to go.

"I don't know about that," she said.

Sam drew back and looked at her. "Are you modest?"

Kate shook her head. "No, but I don't have a shower."

Sam thought about that for a moment. "What do you have?"

She took his hand and pulled him out of the bed with her. "I'll show you."

Kate started to tug him toward the bathroom and then made the mistake of looking back. She stopped in her tracks and forgot, for the time being, where she was going. He stood before her, stark naked, and she was momentarily overcome by the sheer masculine vitality of him.

"You're staring, Katie," he said, and the sound of his voice brought her back to reality. "Do you like what you see?" he asked in a cockily endearing kind of way.

"Yes," she said breathlessly, and then, to cover her embarrassment, she turned and pulled him toward the bathroom. "Here's what I want to show you."

Sam looked at the thing she was pointing at. "Is that a bathtub or a boat?"

Kate laughed. She'd thought the very same thing the first time she'd seen it. Her bathtub was an old claw-footed monster that could easily fit three with room to spare. "I've thought of donating it to the museum. It must be the only one in existence."

"I think we could put it to better use than that," Sam said. "Do you have any juice?"

Kate wrinkled her brow. She'd heard of bathtub gin, but bathtub orange juice? "Yes."

"Don't look at me that way!" Sam said and then

laughed. "I'll get the juice and you fill up the tub. We'll take a long, leisurely bath and sip the juice while we're doing it."

Sam left and Kate began to draw water for the bath. By the time the tub was full, Sam had returned with two enormous glasses filled with ice and orange juice. He set them down next to the tub, took her hand, and helped her into the water.

"Ah, just right," he said, sighing as he settled into the water and leaned against the back of the tub directly opposite from Kate. He picked up his ice-cold glass and began to sip from it. "Drink your juice, Kate," he directed.

Kate picked up her glass and began to sip slowly, all the while watching Sam through the tendrils of steam that rose from the water and made his chestnut locks curl on his forehead.

His foot stroked her thigh lazily, sending a thrill of excitement through her system. The orange juice flowed down her throat, cold and tart, as the water lapped against her body like a warm, liquid, loving caress. She closed her eyes and gave in to the sensations flooding her body. She felt a wave peaking over the tips of her breasts, and when she opened her eyes Sam's face was in front of her, his irises golden orbs with piercing black centers. Her thighs were cradled between his knees.

"I think I've had enough juice," he said.

She met his bold stare. "I'd like one more sip," she replied, and gulped some juice down quickly. It hit the bottom of her throat with an icy blast and shocked her into a hiccup. Sam looked at her skeptically, but she hiccuped again and then a third time.

Sam leaned with his elbow on the edge of the tub

and rested his chin on his hand. "Are you trying to avoid me, Kate?" he questioned.

"No," she said, and then hiccuped again. "I can't stop."

"Hold your breath," he ordered.

She did as she was told, and just when she thought that the spasms had stopped, she hiccuped again. Her eyes rose to his guiltily. "What next?"

"I could scare you," he suggested.

"Not if you warn me first," she answered, and punctuated the end of her sentence with another hiccup.

Sam picked up her glass of juice. "Sip this, backwards."

"Backwards?" Kate asked, bewildered.

"Tilt the glass and sip from the other side."

Kate did as she was told, but she began to laugh at the difficulty of it, and that sent her off into another paroxysm of hiccuping.

"Don't laugh," Sam pleaded.

"I can't help it. It's so funny. Here we are in this tub, and it's so warm and wonderful, and you want to . . . well, you want to . . ." She couldn't say it.

"Make love to you," Sam encouraged.

"Make love to me," she parroted him, "and I've got the hiccups." She burst into laughter again.

"Well, I've got an easy solution to that," he said.

"What?" she asked, and her eyes searched his, wide open and filled with desire.

"I'll just ignore them."

His hands began to caress her body in smooth, soothing strokes. His mouth sought hers and, ignoring the spasms that shook her chest, he kissed her, a long, languorous kiss that almost took her breath away. She wrapped her arms around his neck and drew him closer so that she could feel the hardness of his desire pressed against her inner thigh.

She shivered as his mouth moved down from hers and began to lap at the point where the water ended and her breasts began. She twined her hands in the tangled locks of his steamy hair and lifted her body to his eager mouth.

"Hiccups gone?" Sam asked, his eyes meeting hers in a look that was passionately intense.

"Yes," she murmured. "All gone."

"If you ever get them again, remember that this is the way to get rid of them."

"I'll remember," Kate whispered.

"But only with me," Sam said.

"Only with you," she repeated.

"And only in bathtubs." His lips were hot on her mouth, emblazoning their hungry imprint.

"Only in bathtubs," she answered, hardly knowing what she was saying, mindful only of the sharp plea-sure Sam's lips and hands were giving. Her legs wrapped around his waist as she drew him into herself with a low moan.

She moaned again as she felt the exquisite warmth and fullness of him inside her. She felt totally en-wrapped and consumed by him as he rocked them in the water. Softly slapping waves rolled over them, mimicking the sensuous rhythm of their undulating bodies.

She could feel the heat building within her and within him. They seemed totally as one as they rocked together. And then the heat rushed to her loins, and just as Sam called Kate's name and crushed her to him, it exploded outward like a pulsating ball of fire roaring through her.

Sam's head lay on her breast; he still clutched her fiercely against him, as if he were afraid that she might leave him too soon. Kate stroked his head and hoped that the gesture was as soothing to him as it was to her.

She had never expected this to happen with Sam Davis; in fact, she'd fought against it from the beginning. But now, in the afterglow of their loving, she couldn't remember why she had fought so hard to prevent it. Kate realized suddenly that she was in love with Sam, and her instincts, those little demons that came out of nowhere and that she had tried and tried to ignore, were telling her that the feeling was absolutely and unconditionally mutual. It was almost scary.

But just then Sam raised his head and gave her a look so full of love and so cherishing that her heart filled with happiness and she wasn't frightened anymore.

They had their breakfast in Kate's sunny kitchen, both of them wrapped up in bath towels. Kate lingered over her coffee, almost not wanting to go to the museum, because that meant saying good-bye to Sam. He must have sensed her pensive mood, for he gave her a searching look.

"Happy?" he asked.

She looked over at his face. It had become so dear to her in such a short amount of time.

She nodded. "Yes, I'm happy."

"No regrets?" he questioned.

She shook her head. "None."

"I'm glad." He stood and began to gather up their plates and then placed them in the sink. "But I guess we'd better get going."

"I know," she said.

"What are you up to today?" he asked as they headed back to her room to change into their clothes.

"I've got to pick out paint for the walls and hire the painters. Now that I've got that donation, I can print up some brochures, too. I just wish I knew who gave me that money and why the contributer wants to be anonymous."

Sam gave her a sharp look as he donned his sports jacket.

She laughed. "Don't worry, I wasn't being coy. I don't suspect you anymore."

He approached her with what she could only surmise was an offended look on his face. Noticing that his tie was crooked, she reached up to straighten it.

"I should never have suspected you. You're not the underhanded type."

He didn't say anything, but his face still held its offended expression. She guessed that his feelings were hurt because she had once suspected him.

"Am I forgiven for thinking that you might have been the underhanded type?" she asked.

He wrapped his arms around her and pulled her close. "You're forgiven."

"Let's make a deal, then," Kate said. It had become a kind of code phrase between them.

"All right." He nuzzled her hair with his lips.

"From now on, we'll be completely honest with each other. No more suspicions, okay?"

"Okay, but there's something—"

Kate interrupted him. "I know you're thinking that I may not be able to live up to it—with my past track record and all." She drew away from him and solemnly crossed her heart with her hand like a child. "I swear to be honest and aboveboard from this moment on. Deal?"

Sam smiled, but his grin was rather weak. "Deal."

"Great." She kissed him lightly on the nose. "I've got to get some papers together before I go to work, so you go on ahead."

"All right."

She walked him to the door.

"Are you free for dinner?" he asked.

"I think it can be arranged." She smiled at him impishly.

"I'll call you," he said, and then he was out the door.

On her way over to the museum, Kate thought about how different she was feeling now from the time when she had thought she was in love with David Atwood. Then, each moment had been anxious and unsettling, since she was constantly wondering if David was going to approve of what she did or be angry over something that she didn't do. It was so different with Sam. Today she felt free and happy, as if she'd been released from some kind of private, self-imposed imprisonment. Now it didn't matter what she did or didn't do, because she sensed that with Sam, whatever she did would be fine with him as long as it was fine with her. He had no mental yardstick that he would always be measuring her against.

Kate wondered if that was what love was all about, and decided, as she mounted the steps to the museum, that it must be.

Jane was sitting at her desk, typing, when Kate entered the office.

"You look awfully happy this morning," Jane said. "You must have known that your wish was coming true."

Kate looked at her, perplexed. Did she know about Sam? "What do you mean?"

"Look." Jane pulled the morning's student newspaper off the pile of papers on her desk. "You couldn't tell President Davis off, but someone did."

There, on the front page, was her anonymous letter. She had forgotten all about it. "A letter to the editor? I thought they always put these in the back."

"Not this one," Jane crowed. "Wow, wait till Davis sees this!"

Kate pretended to scan it, and then set it down on Jane's desk with a shaky hand. "Well, I guess that tells him," she said weakly.

"You'd better believe it," Jane replied. "The students are all fired up about that letter. A real controversy is brewing."

Kate headed into her office, hoping that Jane would stay at her desk and not say anything else about the letter. How she wished she had never written it! But Jane followed her in.

"I've already talked to a couple of my friends," Jane said. She was young enough so that she had quite a few friends who were undergraduates at Havenport. "Everyone thinks More Than Half a Brain is the greatest thing to hit Havenport since happy hours. They're going to have rallies and protests and—"

Kate looked at her aghast. "Rallies?"

"Well, yes, of course," Jane said, as if it were obvious. "But it's funny," she said.

Funny was not how Kate would have described it. *Disastrous and horrifying* was more like it.

"Some of the kids think More Than Half a Brain's a hero for telling off Davis, and some of them just don't understand sarcasm. They think that More Than Half a Brain's completely serious about doing away with dining halls and turning off the heat."

"Oh," Kate said, for lack of anything better to say. She had thought that everyone would know that her letter was meant to be a joke—a rather barbed one, but a joke just the same. So much for Swiftian irony; she should have remembered that Swift had been taken literally, too.

"But they're all agreed on one thing," Jane went on.

"What's that?" Kate asked, hardly wanting to know the answer.

"That they've got to find out who More Than Half a Brain is."

Kate shot her a wide-eyed look. "Do they have any clues?" She didn't think that she had left a trail that would lead back to her, but she hadn't exactly planned on all of this happening, so she hadn't taken any precautions.

"Just the envelope the letter came in with More Than Half a Brain's handwriting on it."

"Have you seen it?" Kate asked anxiously. That's all she needed—her own assistant turning her over to the rampaging hordes.

"Nope. The editor's got it and he's doing all the detective work." Jane leaned against the door frame and raised her eyes. "Isn't this exciting? A real controversy on campus. It's like being back in the sixties. I was always sorry I missed all those sit-ins and be-ins and demonstrations. Boy, I can't wait!" Jane buzzed out of the office as if she'd had far too many cups of coffee.

Kate sank into her desk chair, grateful for its soft, leathery assurance. Now she was really in a pickle. That very morning she had sworn always to be honest with Sam. How was she ever going to tell him about this? If things really were heating up as Jane said, the campus was going to be in a complete and total uproar, and Sam was going to have something close to a riot on his hands.

She supposed it was possible that Jane was exaggerating and the whole thing would blow over. Midterms were coming up soon, and most of the students would be a lot more concerned about their grades than rallying around the cause of More Than Half a Brain. But that still didn't get her off the hook. Should she write another letter to the editor and retract her statement? She considered that for a moment. No, that would probably only inflame the students even further; they might think that More Than Half a Brain was being paid off by the administration to change his or her mind.

She thought of calling Helen and asking her advice, but nixed that idea quickly. She didn't think she could admit to Helen that she'd done anything this foolish.

No, the best she could hope for was that the editor of the student newspaper was a poor detective and would soon tire of tracking down More Than Half a Brain. But she had to tell Sam . . .

She picked up her phone and began to dial his

number, then thought better of it and hung up. This was something she would have to do in person. She could tell him at dinner that night; that would be soon enough, and besides, she had so much to do and arrange that day that she really didn't have the time to run over to his office. Kate didn't know whether she was rationalizing or being sensible about postponing her confession, but if she waited until evening, at least she'd have time to think of the best way to break the news to him.

Kate spent the whole morning calling up paint stores, painters, and printers. At noon she decided to run out to some of the hardware stores and look at paint samples. Just as she hit the bottom step of the museum, she heard her name being called.

"Kate! Wait a minute." It was Sam, moving toward her at a fast and frantic pace.

He looked utterly wonderful. His hair was tousled, as if he'd been running his hands through it, and his whole body seemed almost to tremble with vitality. Something must be up.

He placed a hand on her shoulder. "I'm glad I caught up with you." He was a little winded and his breath was coming in ragged bursts. "I can't have dinner with you tonight."

Kate's heart sank. She had really been looking forward to it, and she desperately needed to tell him about More Than Half a Brain.

Sam waved a newspaper in the air. "Have you seen this?" he asked.

Kate didn't even have to look at it to know it was the campus newspaper with her letter on the front page. "Yes. I need to talk to you about something." Confessing to him on the museum steps that she was really More Than Half a Brain wasn't how she had pictured the scene happening, but she figured she might as well tell him now if she wasn't going to be able to tell him at dinner.

"I know. You probably agree with all of it." Sam gave her a wicked grin. "But I can't even talk now. I've got to try to straighten this out before all hell breaks loose."

"That's just what I want to speak to you about..." she began, but Sam wouldn't let her continue.

"I'm sure you have all kinds of wonderful ideas about how to nip this thing in the bud, Katie, but I'm meeting a coalition of students and I'm already late."

"But—"

"Listen, I'll see you tomorrow at that Friends of the Museum meeting." Kate had forgotten about that. It was an annual roundup of all the donors and patrons of the museum, and the president always put in a short appearance.

"Okay, but—"

Sam leaned over and kissed her quickly yet tantalizingly on the mouth. "Rest up tonight, Katie. You're going to need all your strength for tomorrow," he teased with snapping eyes.

Kate merely nodded her head. She didn't think she'd get a moment's worth of rest, and she knew she'd need strength for something completely different from what Sam Davis had in mind.

She watched as he loped across the quadrangle and then her eyes were caught by something strange. Why were all the tree trunks white? She slowly walked toward the nearest cluster of trees, and as she got closer she realized that they were covered with some kind of mimeographed flyer. When she was finally near enough to read one of them, her heart leaped so high and so hard in her chest that she was afraid it had permanently lodged itself in her throat.

WANTED: DEAD OR ALIVE, it said. REWARD FOR THE CAPTURE AND RETURN OF MORE THAN HALF A BRAIN. Kate almost fainted on the spot. The reward was a full case of an expensive imported beer. She knew it was the kind of bait that no undergraduate would be able to resist. As she stood there, a group of students gathered around her.

"Hey, look at this! A whole case of beer!" one of them yelled.

"Holy cow!" said another. "We could have some kind of party with that!"

Kate wanted to shrink into the sidewalk beneath her feet. She was surrounded by bounty hunters.

"Let's do it!" one of them yelled, and then they all tore off in a raucous group, laughing and yelling about how they'd track the culprit down.

Kate remained rooted to the spot. If she had hoped before that the whole thing would just blow over, her hopes were now utterly dashed. A bunch of college kids in competition for a free case of beer would probably have tricks up their sleeves that would put a Wild West bounty hunter to shame.

Chapter 9

Kate was lying on an enormous bed of autumn leaves. She could feel their prickly edges through her clothing, and their dust coated her skin with a fine golden powder. She rolled over onto her stomach and buried her nose in the leaves, trying not to sneeze as she inhaled their rich, almost burnt, earthy smell. It was then that she realized she wasn't alone. Sam was lying next to her. Where had he come from?

The leaves made a delicious crackling noise as he reached over to draw her into his embrace. Her eyes locked with his. Amber inlaid with onyx. He placed his hands on her hips and drew her close, bringing her loins up against his. She buried her nose in the soft wool of his sweater and inhaled his warm, intoxicating smell as his hips moved against her belly in a deeply sensuous rhythm. Then their lips met. He branded her mouth with a kiss so fiery that she was afraid they'd set the leaves aflame.

"Sam, oh, Sam," she moaned. "I love you."

"Kate, I . . ."

Suddenly, there was a crackling noise behind them. Kate looked up to see a young man bearing down upon them, dressed in a deerstalker hat and an inver-

*ness coat, clenching a long-stemmed meershaum pipe
between his teeth.*

*"At last, at last!" he bellowed. "I've found you at
last!"*

*He stood in front of them now. He pointed his pipe
at Kate accusingly. "You're More Than Half a Brain!"*

"No, I'm not," she gasped. "I'm not!"

*He pulled a campus-mail envelope out of his pocket
with a flourish. "This is your handwriting, Kate Burnham. You* are *More Than Half a Brain." He waved
the envelope around in the air.*

*Kate looked at Sam. His eyes were wide with sur-
prise. And then she felt his body slip away from hers.
He was gone, and all she could remember was the
horrible look of betrayal on his face just before he
disappeared.*

*"I'm sorry I have to do this." The young man lit
a match. "For God, for America, for Havenport!" he
exclaimed as he tossed the match on the leaves and
then ran away.*

*Flames began to lick angrily all around her. She
heard bells, or was it a siren? A fire truck was coming.
Would they rescue her in time?*

Briiing! Briiing! Kate sat up sharply. It was the
telephone jangling on her coffee table. She had thrown
herself onto the couch after work, exhausted, and must
have fallen asleep. Her heart was pounding wildly at
being awakened abruptly. Thank heavens. It had only
been a dream and she wasn't about to be incinerated.

She stumbled over to the phone and picked it up
while she took a quick look at her watch. Eleven
o'clock. She'd been asleep for hours.

"Kate?" It was Sam. She'd never been more glad
to hear anyone's voice.

"Yes," she murmured, as she tried to shake the sleep from her brain.

"I miss you," he said simply.

Kate flopped into a chair. She could still see that betrayed look on Sam's face just after he had found out that she was More Than Half a Brain. An enormous lump formed at the base of her throat.

"Are you still there?" he asked.

"Yes, I'm here." Kate drew her knees up to her chest and scrunched down in the chair, shivering. The night air was crisp and she had left all the windows open.

"I'm sorry about dinner tonight, but things have gotten so crazy. I guess you know what's happening."

"Yes," she barely managed to choke out. If anyone should know, she should.

"I'll tell you something, though," he said.

"What?"

"I feel sorry for whoever wrote that letter, that More Than Half a Brain character. The students are so worked up that I fear for his or her life. Half of them want to lynch whoever it is, and the other half want to put More Than Half a Brain on a pedestal. I'd like to... Well, why ruin a perfectly nice conversation?"

Kate cringed. She didn't know for sure what he'd like to do if he found out the real identity of More Than Half a Brain, but she thought she knew what he probably would do: He'd disappear from her life completely. "Maybe it'll all die down soon," she said weakly.

"That's a nice sentiment, Katie, but I don't think mass rallies are in the 'It will all die down soon' category."

"Rallies?" she squeaked.

"They won't tell me where, but don't be surprised if you find students camping out on the museum steps tomorrow. They know about the meeting."

Kate's stomach did the most peculiar thing. It lurched, flipped over twice, and then settled somewhere in the vicinity of her throat. It was quite a disturbing sensation. She couldn't say a word with her stomach clutching her vocal chords.

"Well, that's enough of that," Sam said. "I called because you said there was something you wanted to tell me."

"I did?" Kate decided that if she pretended she had never said it, Sam might believe she hadn't. There was no way she was going to tell him she was More Than Half a Brain tonight. That dream had seemed too real.

"You did. And I bet I know what it is." His voice was like a caress to her ears.

"What?" She decided to let him fill in the blanks.

"That you're as wildly attracted to me as I am to you and that you can't bear to be without me," he said, and laughed lightly.

Kate felt a warm shiver course through her system. "That's right," she said. "How did you guess?" She was surprised at how easily she was able to slip away from the truth. Since when had she become such a master of deceit? Her mother had always said that Kate was a terrible liar because what she felt was always written all over her face. Thank goodness for the telephone!

"It's not that late; I could still come over," Sam said in a very persuasive tone of voice.

"Oh, Sam, I'd love that, but I'm so tired." At last she'd said something that was true.

"Are you sure you don't have iron-poor blood or something, Katie? For a young woman, you seem to have an inordinate number of tired spells," he bantered.

Kate couldn't help laughing. "I spent most of the day on the phone with paint stores. Have you ever tried to describe the difference between ivory and cream?"

"No." He chuckled. "That's hard. But I could describe your eyes."

"You already have. You compared them to a storm-tossed sea." Their flirtation was fun, and Kate was forgetting for the moment what she was concealing with it.

"That's only when you're angry. Last night they were like lapis lazuli."

Kate remembered the previous night. Suddenly his presence seemed so powerful that she could almost swear he was in the room with her, pressed up against her in the most intimate of embraces.

"And your hair. It's like finely polished copper, it's so smooth and shiny."

"Yours is like a horse's," she whispered.

"Thanks a lot!" Sam nearly choked.

"I mean a stallion," she protested. "A wild chestnut stallion."

"That's better. Are you sure you don't want this horse to gallop on over?" He said it with a cowboy's western twang.

It was easy to flirt with him on the phone, but Kate knew she wouldn't be able to hide her guilty face if he came over. She still wasn't prepared, if she ever would be, to tell him her secret. She didn't say anything.

"I guess that means no." Kate could hear the disappointment in his voice and her heart gave the slightest of quakes. "Well, maybe you're right. But I'll see you tomorrow.

"Yes. Tomorrow."

"Good night, then, Katie. Sleep well."

"You, too," she said, placing the receiver softly in its cradle.

Kate was surprised when she awoke in the morning still curled up in the chair. She thought only the innocent slept the sleep of babes.

When Kate got to the museum that morning, patrons and trustees were already milling about in the grand neo-Gothic sculpture hall. A table had been set up with coffee urns, teapots, and trays and trays of pastries. The museum volunteers, genteel older ladies dressed in tweeds and wools, seemed, as usual, to have everything under control. Sam hadn't arrived yet.

It had always been the president's custom to make an entrance halfway through the meeting and then give a short speech welcoming everyone to the museum. Kate wondered what he would say, now that it had become official policy to abandon the museum. Whatever he said, she was sure he'd handle the situation gracefully, and no one would feel the least bit slighted. Even she was beginning to see the sense in his decision. If only she'd seen it before...

Helen was standing in front of the table and motioned to Kate to join her.

"Kate, you're looking wonderful," she exclaimed, her eyes sparkling knowingly.

"I took your advice," Kate said as she poured herself a cup of rich, brown coffee and turned it to beige with a splash of cream.

"You took a chance, right?" Helen's face had a certain I-told-you-so look about it, but in the nicest way.

"I did. I think it's the best advice I've ever been given." She gave Helen a warm smile. "Thank you."

"No charge," Helen said, and laughed. "I take it the man who put that lovely glow on your face is due to arrive at any moment," she teased.

Kate nodded. "I have to talk to you about something." She had made up her mind the night before, right after she had said good night to Sam, to talk to Helen about her predicament. Embarrassing or not, she had to talk to someone about it, because she was in a complete quandary as to how to break the news to Sam that she was More Than Half a Brain.

"Shall we retire to the coatroom?" Helen asked.

They were on their way out of the sculpture hall when a courtly, gray-haired older man stopped Helen with a smile and a handshake. It was the trustee who had been speaking with Sam the night of Helen's exhibition opening.

"Chilton. How nice to see you," Helen said. "Have you met Kate Burnham?"

Chilton Harrison turned to Kate with a bright look in his eyes. "No, we haven't met. How do you do?"

Kate shook his hand and was ready to withdraw hers when he placed his other hand on top of it and clasped it warmly.

"It's nice to finally meet you," he said.

Kate wondered what he meant by that.

"Kate!" It was Alex Jensen with another trustee in tow. "I want you to meet Mr. Winthrop. He thinks he has something in his attic you might be interested in." Kate said good-bye to Helen and Chilton Harrison, knowing that now she'd have to wait until after the meeting to talk to Helen. She went off with Alex and Mr. Winthrop and then Alex left them alone to talk together.

Apparently, from what she could tell from his description, Winthrop had an old chest in his attic that might be a hand-carved relic from the seventeenth century. It had been passed down through the family for as long as Mr. Winthrop could remember. Kate suspected that it was authentic. She arranged an appointment to look at it sometime during the week, and then she made idle conversation with Winthrop until she heard Alex clapping his hands for attention. The meeting was getting under way.

Kate smiled at Mr. Winthrop and then moved to the other side of the room to take her place with the other curators, slipping into a folding chair next to Helen. Just as Alex began his speech, Sam entered the hall.

He stood next to one of the marble columns that flanked the doorway and she saw his eyes searching the crowd for her. When he finally saw her, his face lit up and he tilted his head slightly to acknowledge that he had found what he was looking for. Kate nodded back and smiled nervously. She wondered if he would be so pleased to see her after he learned that she was responsible for the More Than Half a Brain brouhaha.

Alex finished his speech, everyone applauded, and

then he introduced Sam. Sam walked to the front of the crowd and began to speak. He started off with a few words of welcome, outlined some of the activities that the museum would be involved in during the coming year, and then got down to the real business of his speech.

"I'm sure that some of you are already aware of the college's new policy toward the museum."

There was some nodding of heads and a bit of uneasy shifting in seats by a few of the trustees.

"I'm also sure that some of you aren't happy about it."

His candid remark brought forth nervous laughter from the crowd.

"I'm not, either," he said. "I'm not immune to the beauty and worth of art"—he paused dramatically— "as some may think. But I found I had to make a difficult choice. I could either allow the college to continue to support the museum and run the risk of folding, or..." He stopped speaking momentarily to allow the murmuring of some of the people in the crowd to subside. Kate suspected that quite a few of them didn't know just how serious the financial plight of the college was. "... or I could make some budget cuts so that the college won't fold. I chose the latter."

Several heads nodded in agreement. They could see the sense in what he said.

"What that means," he continued, "is that each one of you becomes that much more important to the museum. We can only hope that you'll be just as generous in your support as you've always been." He grinned engagingly. "And maybe just a smidgen more generous."

Everyone laughed. Sam was winning them over.

Kate had to admire his tact and charm. He was in a difficult position, yet walked the very fine line with great delicacy. She wouldn't be surprised if the money started to pour in.

"I'm hoping that this will be the beginning of a new era for the museum. With your help, I'm sure we can get over the hump. And don't forget that all your contributions are tax-deductible."

This seemed to crack everyone up for some reason. There was applause and even a few cheers and shouts of "Hear, hear."

But when the ovation died down, Kate heard another noise. It sounded as if it were coming from outside; if her ears weren't fooling her, she was hearing a large number of young voices chanting an as yet indistinguishable phrase over and over again.

The room was silent. Kate saw Alex look at Sam questioningly and then Sam headed out of the room toward the entrance foyer of the museum. The trustees and patrons began to mill about and then headed after Sam. Everyone wanted to know what the commotion was. Kate followed the crowd to the front door and then slithered through the bottleneck that had formed in front of it. The chanting was getting louder and louder, and finally, as she reached the entrance to the museum, she was able to distinguish what the crowd was saying.

"Long live Half a Brain," they kept repeating.

Her eyes took in a crowd of rowdy students that had to number in the hundreds. Their fresh faces were bright with fanatical zeal. Some of them were carrying placards, and they waved them about in such an abandoned fashion that Kate was afraid several pairs of eyes were in distinct danger of being poked out. One of the placards said LONG LIVE MORE THAN HALF A BRAIN, OUR HERO, another said DEATH TO ALL PURITANS: and a third, which seemed to have taken its cue from a bumper sticker, said ART IS FOR LOVERS.

Kate caught Sam's eye. He looked distressed. He pushed open the glass door and walked out onto the front steps. The noise of the crowd died down as Sam stood there, waiting for silence. Some of the friends of the museum gathered behind him, whether to show their support or satisfy their curiosity, Kate didn't know. She stayed within the open doorway of the museum, wishing that she could turn and run back in; but there were so many people crowded together behind her that she was trapped where she was.

"I know you're not happy with these budget cuts..." Sam began. The crowd unanimously agreed with his first statement with a burst of applause and jeers. "...but I have no choice. If any of you have any ideas, I'd be happy to listen to them." The crowd was silent. "Where's your leader?" Sam asked. "Where is More Than Half a Brain?" That seemed to deflate the throng.

Kate cringed in the doorway. "I'm right here," she said miserably to herself.

"We'll find 'em," one of the students yelled. This seemed to cheer everyone up. There was a great deal of cheering and hooting about how they were hot on the trail of their leader.

But before Sam could say anything else, Kate heard the sounds of a marching band. And then she saw, coming around the corner of the museum at a breakneck pace, a raggedy band dressed in makeshift colonial costumes playing a free-form version of "Yankee Doodle." They were carrying their own signs: DEATH

TO MORE THAN HALF A BRAIN, HALF A BRAIN? NO
BRAIN!, AND HALF A BRAIN WHERE ARE YOU? STAND
UP AND FIGHT LIKE A MAN/WOMAN!

As the two groups merged, Kate saw that the inevitable was happening. If Sam was lucky, the pushing and shoving wouldn't turn into punching and
fighting, but for a few moments she sensed that the
situation was tense. Sam waited for the crowd to set-
tle, and then he began to speak again.

"I know you're all here for a good cause," he began. "You all care about our college."

This set off an enormous amount of cheering, including a quick rendition of one of the Havenport
football team's fight songs. In the very back of the
crowd, Kate could barely see a group of cheerleaders,
dressed in their orange and green outfits, flailing madly
about with their pom-poms. She wondered which side
they were on and then decided that they were probably
remaining neutral, if only so they could cheer more
often by cheering for everything.

"As I said before, I'm eager to hear whatever ideas
you might have about improving our situation at Havenport. With one condition."

"What's that?" someone in the crowd yelled.

"Since I can't speak to each and every one of you
about this, I think it's more practical to speak to just
one person: your leader. I'll talk to More Than Half
a Brain. No one else."

"What if we can't find 'em?" one of the students
piped up.

Sam thought about that for a minute, then made
his reply. "I think if More Than Half a Brain really
believes in what they're saying, he or she will come
forth. Until your leader is willing to meet me, one on

one, we won't get anywhere. So"—Sam paused and then flashed a wide smile—"take me to your leader!"

The crowd let out a loud whoop. Kate thought it sounded like an Indian war cry. And the students took off en masse, probably to regroup somewhere else and form a posse. She leaned weakly against the stone wall of the entryway.

The patrons and trustees of the museum gathered around Sam. Several of the men pounded him on the back and congratulated him on how he had handled the crowd. He looked over at Kate, as if hoping to see a sign of approval in her eyes, but the best she could do was flash him a rather wan smile. Helen came up to her and placed her hand on Kate's shoulder.

"You look a little upset," she said. "Are you worried about Sam?"

"Not exactly," Kate replied.

"Oh?" Helen shot her a questioning look. "What then?"

"Shall we retire to the cloakroom?"

They headed into the museum, but when they arrived at the cloakroom they found that it was filled with trustees and patrons trying to find their coats. Everyone was in a state of confusion after the excitement of the student rally. Kate looked at Helen, rolled her eyes, grabbed her hand, and propelled her into one of the empty conference rooms.

She closed the door behind them and then collapsed into an empty chair and covered her face with her hands.

"Kate, what's wrong?" Helen asked, her voice filled with concern.

"You're not going to believe this." Kate shook her

head. "You simply are not going to believe this."

"Tell me first, and then we'll decide," Helen encouraged.

Kate looked up at Helen. The older woman's face was expectant and receptive. "Helen," she said, "I'm More Than Half a Brain."

Kate heard the sharp intake of Helen's breath, and then Helen, too, flopped down into a chair.

"Unfortunately, I believe it."

"You do?" Kate asked.

Helen crossed her legs calmly and dangled a shoe from an outstretched big toe. "I had my suspicions. The letter seemed like you might have written it. It was funny and charming and had a familiar bite to it. What did you do? Send it out before you found out who Sam really was?"

Kate was surprised at how well Helen had figured everything out. "Yes. But I had no idea it was going to turn into this," she said miserably. She rested her cheek against the palm of her hand and then propped her elbow up on the arm of the chair. "What should I do?" she asked quietly.

"Tell him," Helen answered simply.

"What if he never wants to speak to me again afterward?"

"I doubt that will happen. He'll probably think the whole thing is very funny. Besides, at least if you're More Than Half a Brain, he'll know he's dealing with someone who's reasonable, instead of the kook he probably *thinks* More Than Half a Brain is."

Kate realized that Helen had a good point there. She was beginning to feel a lot better about the situation now that it didn't seem so hopeless. Maybe there was a happy ending to this miserable mixup.

She smiled at Helen, and then she heard a knock on the door. "Come in," she said.

The door opened and Sam poked his head into the room. "Alex said he saw you two disappear in here. Am I interrupting anything important?" He shut the door behind him.

"No." Helen laughed. "Just girl talk." She was a marvelous actress, Kate thought wistfully.

Sam turned to Kate. He looked so handsome standing there that her breath caught momentarily in her chest and she had to force herself to exhale slowly. His hair was tousled and windswept and his eyes were bright from the excitement of the rally. "How'd I do?" he asked anxiously.

"Wonderfully," Kate said. "You're a born leader." She hadn't meant for it to come out sarcastically, but from the look on Sam's face she could tell that it had.

He flashed her a puzzled look. "I wish that More Than Half a Brain would put in an appearance. My mysterious adversary is a coward, don't you think?"

Kate met Helen's eyes with a guilty look. They exchanged glances so quickly that Kate was sure Sam couldn't have detected it. "Maybe he or she has good reasons to lie low," she said.

"Well, it can't last much longer," Sam said. "Those kids are determined to track down whoever it is."

Helen got up from her chair. "I'll be on my way now," she said. Kate figured that Helen was making an exit so that Kate could begin her confession, but she had no intention of telling Sam now. Not in the wake of that rally. She'd tell him later, she promised herself.

"I'll go with you," Sam said to Helen, surprising Kate. "I just wanted to see if Kate is free for dinner."

He looked at her. "Are you?"

She nodded her head.

"Good. I'll pick you up at seven."

Kate nodded again, then watched uneasily as Helen and Sam left. Dinner. At seven. She'd tell him after dinner. Yes, she would, she vowed. But it was going to be the hardest thing she'd ever done.

Chapter 10

KATE WONDERED WHAT a woman was supposed to wear for a confession. She stood in front of her opened closet and scrutinized the dresses, blouses, skirts, and sweaters, wondering which combination would be the most appropriate. Should she wear all black? That would look repentant enough. Or should she dress in brilliant, blazing red to show that she was sorry she'd made a mistake but not ashamed? What about a black skirt and a red sweater? That might strike just the right note of compromise.

She pulled a fluffy crimson angora sweater off a hanger and then, clutching it in her hand, threw herself down on the bed, pressed the soft material to her face, and sighed. She wondered what Sam would say when she told him. He'd probably be furious over the trouble she had caused. Why had she been so impulsive?

Well, there was no use in thinking about her impulses now. The milk had been spilled and it was time to figure out the best way to mop it up. Kate rolled over onto her back and gazed up at the ceiling. She stared at a small crack near the light fixture for such a long time that it split in two; then she saw two cracks and two lights. Suddenly, a little bell rang in her head.

It had something to do with that theory Sam had about being two different people—the professional Radley and the private Sam. If she could appeal to the Sam side of his character with her confession, she knew he'd find the situation funny in a way that the Radley side wouldn't. She would ask him, as Sam, to listen to her confession, and, as Sam, he'd have to think it was at least mildly amusing. Or so she hoped.

Half an hour later, she was dressed and waiting for Sam's knock on the door. Instead of the black skirt she'd planned on wearing, she'd changed her mind and slipped on a yellow one. With yellow stockings and red shoes to match her red sweater, she felt almost cheerful.

When the doorbell rang, she leaped up and ran to the door, she was so anxious to confess and get it over with. She threw open the door.

Sam stood there, wearing jeans and a crew-neck sweater instead of his usual academic tweeds and wools. He looked her over from head to toe and then whistled under his breath. "Red and yellow catch a fellow," he said with a grin.

He passed through the open doorway and entered her apartment, moving so quickly that he left a stiff breeze in his wake. "Haven't you ever heard that phrase?" he asked when he noticed her puzzled expression.

"No." Kate shut the door after him. Why was he dressed so casually? She'd expected, since it was Saturday night, that they'd go to a restaurant that required more formal clothing than he was wearing.

Now he was pacing back and forth in the living room.

"I thought we'd do something different tonight," he said as he rounded the curve between her sofa and a chair and headed back.

"Would you like to have a seat until we do?" Kate asked. His pacing was making her even more nervous than she'd been before he'd arrived, and she hadn't thought that was possible.

Sam looked at her. His eyes had a distracted, cloudy look to them, like autumnal haze. "Oh," he said. "Of course." He plopped down onto the sofa. "Do I get a hello kiss now?" He reached out, captured her hand in his, and drew her down onto the sofa next to him.

"All right," Kate said, and pecked him chastely.

"You call that a kiss?" He seized her shoulders, clutched her roughly, and gave her a passionate kiss. "That's better," he said with a smile.

Kate pulled back and looked at him. What had gotten into him since she'd seen him that afternoon?

Sam laughed. "Did I grow a third eye or something? You're looking at me in the most peculiar way."

"Have you had too much coffee today?" she asked. "You seem a little . . . well, elated." That was an understatement.

"I am," he said, and jumped up, beaming. "I'm very elated." He stood in front of her with a big smile on his face.

Kate wished she could share his enthusiasm. "Why?" She would have thought that the student rally had put him in a bad mood. His campus was close to anarchy and he seemed oblivious to it all.

"Well, first of all, I'm in love with a very beautiful woman."

Kate blushed.

"And second, this More Than Half a Brain business is a godsend."

Kate did a double take. A godsend? She had thought it was a disaster. "You'd better explain yourself. I'm completely lost."

He sat back down. "Well, when President Simpson and I had a talk before he left, he warned me that Havenport was a very apathetic campus. He said that the students didn't seem to care about anything but getting good grades. It worried me, because I think that students should be involved in all sorts of things. I mean, education is more than just academics."

"Yes?" Kate encouraged him.

He continued, "But I didn't know how to get them involved. Then this More Than Half a Brain thing came along and now they're very much involved."

"But," Kate reminded him, "they're involved in protesting against you!"

"I know, but at least they're thinking."

"Thinking about overthrowing you," Kate said.

Sam laughed. "No, Kate, that's wrong. They're involved in thinking of ways in which to make Havenport a better place to be."

Trust Sam, Kate thought to herself, to come up with such an unconventional way of looking at the situation.

"If I had tried, I couldn't have thought up anything as good as More Than Half a Brain to mobilize them."

Kate looked at Sam out of the corner of her eye. A dim premonition of doom was beginning to dawn in her mind. Almost all he'd spoken about so far this evening was Havenport.

"Who are you tonight, if you don't mind my asking?" she asked.

Sam looked at her as if he'd been caught up short. "I hope you don't mind," he apologized, "but tonight I'm Radley."

Kate put her hand over her face and crumpled onto the couch. So much for well-thought-out plans, she joked to herself.

"Is there something wrong with that?" Sam asked. "I know you like Sam better, but I have a certain plan." He looked at her coaxingly.

Kate smiled bravely. "No, that's fine. I like Radley well enough," she said, and then babbled on about unimportant matters while, in her mind, a little angel and a little devil began to argue. The little angel kept saying that she should tell Sam right away that she was More Than Half a Brain, and the little devil kept trying to cover the angel's mouth with her hand, reminding her that there was always tomorrow. The devil won.

"Enough of this fascinating small talk," Sam finally said. "Let's go to dinner." Without waiting for her assent, he propelled her out the door, down the stairs, and into his car.

As he drove along at a breakneck pace toward a destination unknown, Kate wondered how it was she had ever managed to get herself into such a wacky situation with Sam. Normally, she was a very level-headed, serious, career-oriented woman. Was this what happened when a person fell in love?

A few minutes later, Sam pulled into the parking lot of a hamburger stand. A gaudy red neon sign told her that she'd be dining at Danny's. In the back of her mind, Kate remembered Jane telling her that that was the place where Havenport students "hung out," and that certainly seemed to be the case tonight. There were enough cars to fill a minor shopping mall, and kids were leaning against fenders, sitting on hoods, and strolling from car to car while someone's portable tape player blared a song that seemed to have everyone bouncing on their toes.

Kate turned to Sam with an incredulous look on her face. "Is this where we're having dinner?"

"Yep," he said. "You have your choice of hamburger, cheeseburger, or double cheeseburger. The menu's not too elaborate, but at least you don't have the problem of struggling to make up your mind."

"Does this fit into that plan you mentioned earlier?" Kate asked. She had thought they were going to have a quiet evening together, one during which they could talk and get to know one another better. Hamburgers at a takeout joint just didn't seem to fit the bill.

"It does," Sam said. "Now that the lines of communication are open between me and the students, I want to keep them open. What better way than to be seen at a place where they go?"

Kate had to admit to herself, grudgingly, that he was right. If Sam wanted to use the More Than Half a Brain issue—turn it around to suit his own purposes—then he couldn't have chosen a better strategy.

"You don't mind, do you?" he asked, and reached over to touch her hand.

Kate was surprised that in the midst of a parking lot, surrounded by kids and noise, the mere touch of Sam's hand would have the ability to seal them off from everyone else as if they were in their own private, intimate world. But for the briefest of moments, the warm pressure of his fingers upon her own did just that.

She laughed. "Not at all. I love cheeseburgers."

"Well, then, let's go." Sam got out of the car and Kate followed suit. They headed over to the takeout window.

Sam ordered, and as they waited for their burgers and french fries and onion rings and sodas, Kate noticed some of the students nudging each other and whispering. Obviously, they had seen Sam.

When he picked up their order and headed back to the car with her, Kate heard on of the students yell, "Hey, President Davis, you eat here, too?"

Sam turned to the young man who had asked him the question. "Sure. Best burgers in town."

"All right!" the youth said.

Sam set the cardboard box of food down on the hood of his car. "Okay if we eat here?"

"Sure," Kate said. "Okay if I sit on the hood?"

Sam nodded, smiling. His eyes seemed to be thanking her for going along with his plan.

She smiled back at him. "I've always enjoyed dining alfresco."

The young man who had spoken to Sam now approached with a group of chums in tow.

"This is a nice car," he said. "What year?"

"Nineteen fifty-seven," Sam replied.

"I dig the fins," he commented.

"They're pretty good," Sam agreed as he bit into his hamburger. "How's the search for your leader going?" he asked.

Kate, in the middle of a swallow, almost choked. A vision of herself in handcuffs, being led with a chain, flashed through her head. She banished it and continued to chew.

"Well, we're narrowing it down," the student said. "We think it's probably a woman."

Kate's stomach lurched and then righted itself. She guessed that wasn't so bad. At least half the human race was female.

"Oh, why's that?" Sam said.

"Well, the handwriting on the envelope looked like a woman's," the student said. "And we think that she's probably artistically inclined."

Sam shot Kate a quick, amused glance. "You don't say," he remarked.

"Yep. It was very nice handwriting. Very neat."

"Hmmm," Sam murmured.

The student watched as Sam ate some of his french fries. The young man's face was pensive. Obviously, he had something on his mind and he wasn't sure if he could ask it.

"President Davis," he said finally, "may I ask you a question?"

"Shoot," Sam answered.

"What if we can't find More Than Half a Brain? You say that you'll speak with no one else, but what if that person doesn't want to come forward?"

"Well," Sam said, "I'm not inflexible. I'd like to talk to your leader, but if no one comes forth, you can choose a proxy to speak for More Than Half a Brain . . . to speak for the students, I mean. You have to decide among yourselves what you want to do, though. I can't decide for you."

This seemed to set the student's mind at ease. "We're working on some ideas."

"Good," Sam said as he crumpled up the paper his

hamburger had been wrapped in. "When you're ready, just let me know."

"Okay," he said.

Sam looked at Kate. "Ready?" he asked.

Kate nodded her head.

"Let me get rid of this stuff." Sam took the wrappings from her meal and walked over to a trash barrel.

Kate watched the students looking at him fondly. Apparently, his strategy had worked and he had won their trust. She wondered how her confession would change things, but decided to think about that later. Right now all she wanted to do was enjoy the crisp fall evening and Sam's company.

Half an hour later, they were back in her apartment, sipping brandy and listening to a Joni Mitchell record on the stereo. The lights were low, and through an open window Kate could see a waning moon glowing orange in a cobalt sky. Sam was stretched out on the couch, lying with his head in her lap while she stroked his chestnut hair. The brandy made her feel warm and happy, the golden lights made the room cozy and intimate, and the light pressure of his head resting in her lap was comforting and exciting at the same time.

They were both humming along to the song that was playing, occasionally singing the lyrics when they could remember them and laughing when one of them fudged a word. The mood was so intimate, so warm and loving, that Kate hated to interrupt it. But she knew that the time had come. Before she could say a word, though, Sam began to speak.

"I wish that More Than Half a Brain character would come forward . . ." he said.

Kate's jaw dropped. She didn't believe in mental telepathy, but what Sam had just said was uncanny.

She was too shocked to say anything.

He continued: ". . . although I'm beginning to think that no such person exists."

"Who wrote the letter, then?" Kate managed to croak out.

"Maybe a group of students got together and did it for a lark, I don't know. But if they don't come forward, it just makes it more difficult for the students who really want to work this thing out."

Sam's hand had dropped off the edge of the couch and was now caressing Kate's calf. The back of her knee seemed particularly sensitive to the persuasive pressure of his fingertips. It tingled with every stroke of his hand.

Kate took a deep breath and then plunged in. "I'm More Than Half a Brain," she said softly.

Sam's head rustled in her lap, and then he pivoted his body so that he was staring straight up at her. After a moment, he burst out laughing.

Sam reached up and drew her face down closer to his. "I think that's very sweet, Katie, trying to solve my problems for me, but you really shouldn't claim credit where credit isn't due."

"I'm not," Kate moaned. Their interchange was beginning to border on the absurd, she thought. Here she was, finally telling him the truth, and he refused to believe it!

"But anonymous letters just aren't your style, Katie. You're too straightforward, too honest. That's what I love about you." He reached up and tweaked her nose as if she were a schoolgirl.

Kate felt horrible. How could she continue to insist she'd done something that he wouldn't believe she was capable of doing; and even worse, how could she admit to being a devious anonymous-letter writer when he was convinced that she was the soul of honesty?

She remained silent, staring down into her lap. The little devil inside her had won again.

Suddenly, Sam sat up and drew her into his arms. "You must really care for me to make up such a ridiculous story," he said as he began to kiss her.

No, Kate was saying to herself, I'm what's ridiculous, not the story. But despite the moroseness of her mood she began to respond to his lips.

There was something about Sam's lips that made a response to them inevitable. Perhaps it was the softness or the moist fullness of them, or perhaps it was the sultry way he had of moving them across hers and nibbling at the edges of her mouth. Whatever the reason, Kate found herself succumbing to their pleasures.

"I've been missing you," he murmured as his hands reached up inside her sweater and he ran his palms across the globes of her breasts.

Kate shivered. "I've been missing you," she echoed, in between his ardent kisses.

"I've been thinking about this ever since the last time." His hands continued to tantalize her breasts as his fingers teased the nipples into aching hardness.

"Me, too," Kate said in a tiny, whispery voice. Any disquieting thoughts, any thoughts at all, had vanished completely. She felt only an ever-increasing desire to be joined with him in the most intimate of ways.

He eased her down on the couch, so that she was lying with her back to the cushion, and then fitted himself into the narrow space left, pressing into the curve of her lap. He was unmistakably aroused.

And so was Kate. She could feel the place between her thighs begin to throb with anticipation. She had never before felt so desired—or so desirous.

"Lovely, lovely Kate," Sam whispered as he traced her closed eyelids with a fingertip.

Playfully, she lifted her head and snapped at his finger, taking it between her teeth and squeezing it ever so gently.

"Ah, she bites," he murmured. "But I bite back." He pressed his lips against her neck and then nipped at the exposed skin there. A shiver of excitement ran down her spine. "What else do you do?" he asked suggestively.

"This," she answered, and nipped at his earlobe.

"I like that; do it again." His breath was hot against her cheek.

She obeyed his command and he moaned with pleasure, squirming against her to heighten her excitement. And then she felt him slipping away. He fell off the couch.

"This sofa is cramping my style," he said ruefully as he rubbed his shoulder. "But I've got an easy solution to that."

"What?" Kate asked breathlessly.

"This," he said. He stood up, bent over, and gathered her up into his arms. Carrying her like some precious cargo, he headed for the bedroom.

He set her down on the bed and tumbled down next to her, never letting her leave, even for a second, the warm embrace of his arms.

The kissing began again, only this time more intensely. Sam's tongue forced itself past her lips and explored her mouth lazily. He rolled her over onto her back and covered her with his body while his fingers stroked her hair. Kate was growing more and more overwhelmed by his hands, his mouth, the way he moved against her, convincing her that he desired her, completely and with no reservations.

She opened her eyes for just a moment and saw him, eyes closed, with an expression on his face that was fierce and yet at the same time tender, and she wondered just what it was about him that made her love him so. But before she could consider that any further, he took her attention away from her thoughts and focused it almost excruciatingly on her body.

One hand moved, with tantalizing slowness, up the tender flesh of her inner thigh until it reached the part of her that he knew would crave his touch the most. There his hand rested, the slight pressure of it promising the pleasure that she knew would follow.

Then he took her hand in his own and drew it down below his waist and pressed it against the hardness of his own desire. It was a simple, primitive gesture that inflamed Kate more than any kiss or caress he could have given. She moaned. And then, hardly knowing what she was doing, but guided by some feeling that seemed to go beyond mere emotion and had to be instinctive, she drew down the zipper of his jeans and freed what had been trapped beneath them. A moan caught in his throat.

She began to stroke him. He was perfectly smooth and hard beneath her fingers, and as her hand caressed the full length of him, she marveled at just how perfectly he was wrought, both to give and receive pleasure. Another moan erupted from Sam's throat.

He drew away from her quickly, whispering her name in quick, heavy gasps. He pulled her sweater off with one impatient but graceful sweep of his hand,

and then unzipped her skirt and slipped that off just as quickly. With trembling hands he unhooked her bra and slid it out from under her. Her hose and panties were removed in a flash, and then she was completely naked beneath the blazing fires of his amber eyes.

Reaching up, he pulled off his sweater and shirt at once. Expecting that he would lie at her side, Kate was surprised when he remained kneeling, gazing at her as if he was so intoxicated by the sight that he was incapable of movement. She reached out to him, and as their hands met he drew her up to him so that they were both kneeling on the bed, wrapped in each other's arms.

She laid her head on his shoulder. He placed his hand on the back of her neck and pressed her deeper into the hollow between his shoulder and throat, murmuring her name over and over as if it were an incantation. She gripped his back, loving the strong, masculine feel of his muscles, and pushed herself to him, her breasts flattening against his hard chest. She felt as if she could never be close enough to him no matter how close she got. And then she wished she could crawl inside his skin, and he into hers, so there would be nothing between them—so that they could be of one body, one unity of love.

Tenderly, he pressed her down on the bed. Propped up on his elbows, he slid his body over hers in a slow rhythm so that their flesh touched, but just barely. He was teasing her, but she had come to expect and even relish it, because the teasing only built up her desire for him. She squirmed beneath him and then wrapped her legs around his waist and pulled him close.

"Now I've caught you," she whispered against his probing mouth.

"You caught me a long time ago, Katie," he said. "I'm the one who's done all the chasing."

"But you have me now," she said with a tightened throat. If only he knew just how true that was, and how important it was for her to remain that way.

"But I think you still need some persuading," he whispered tantalizingly in her ear.

"No, no, I don't," she replied, gasping out the words. Her excitement was building to a fever pitch with every gyration he made against her.

He placed a hand over her mouth. "Don't argue with me, Katie. Let me win this one."

Even if she had wanted to argue, Kate wouldn't have been able to. She was past rational thought by now. Sam slipped his hips between her thighs and then found the place he was looking for. She felt the hard, hot length of him pressing against the dewy flower of her womanhood. But he wasn't seeking an entrance to its warm center; instead he was lingering there, probing and pressing until she thought she'd go mad from the sensations that coursed through her body.

Sam must have felt the same, because suddenly he decided that it was time to end his tarrying. With an almost savage thrust, he plunged into her, taking her by surprise and flooding her entire being with a feeling so pure and complete that she had to scream his name just to assure herself that she hadn't left earth behind in a frenzied flight through starry skies. But when she came back down, Sam was still out there, beckoning to her with his thrusts and sensuous movements to follow him again.

Hours later, they lay in one another's arms, caressing idly and kissing languidly and deeply. Kate had never known that loving could feel so extraordinary or that as a woman she could feel so complete. And yet, now that she had returned from her passionate voyage, reality had crept back into her mind. She hadn't been able to convince Sam before that she had been the writer of the anonymous letter, but perhaps she could now.

"Sam?"

"Mmm," he answered, stroking her hair with a reassuring hand.

"I did write that letter, you know."

"Katie, go to sleep. You're babbling." He placed his fingertips on her eyelids and pressed them gently down to meet her lower lashes. "Sleep, Kate. Whatever it is can wait until the morning."

Kate, exhausted, did as she was told.

On Sunday morning Kate awoke lazily to a sun-filled room. She threw her arm across the bed, expecting to come across Sam's sleeping form, but instead she discovered only the hollow his body had left there. Had he gone without saying good-bye? But before she even had a chance to wonder, she heard the front door of her apartment close softly, and looking up at her bedroom doorway, she saw Sam poised in the entrance with a copy of *The New York Times* and a bag of groceries.

She sat up quickly.

Sam raised his hand. "Stay there. Sundays are for breakfast in bed." He went out to the kitchen.

Kate fluffed up her pillow, put her head back, and reveled in the sheer laziness of not having to lift a finger. Soon Sam was back with a trayful of scrambled eggs, juice, and steaming coffee. She smiled.

He looked at her and sighed. "What I'll do just for a smile," he said.

"Is it that important to you?" she asked softly.

"The most important thing in the world," he replied. "Don't you agree?"

She looked at his face. It was so sincere, and shone with so much love, that all she could do was nod.

They ate their breakfast in a companionable silence, looking at each other occasionally and grinning like children. After Kate had left David Atwood, she had thought that all those silly songs that spoke of the power of love to change the world, or at least to change someone's life, were a lot of sentimental hogwash. She'd thought that love was just an illusion, a vague, elusive thing that could only be yearned for and never obtained, and so she had decided never to try to capture it again. Now she was realizing the folly of her assumption, because here, with Sam, love had become a very real thing, so real that she could almost swear it was flowing in the air around them, touching them with golden warmth like the sunlight pouring in through her window.

The rest of the day passed in a golden Indian-summer haze. They dawdled over the paper and then dressed. Sam suggested that they drive out to a park on the outskirts of Havenport and walk through the leaves. Kate couldn't imagine a more pleasant way to spend the afternoon.

As they were slowly kicking their way down a leaf-strewn path, Sam began to talk.

"Did you notice that article in *The New York Times Magazine* about colleges and funding?" he asked.

Kate shook her head. She hadn't read *The New York Times Magazine;* she always saved it to read later in the week.

"It was very interesting. It gave me some good ideas." His voice became excited. "I'd never even thought of arranging a fund-raising event, but that's just what a small college in Kansas did, and it was quite successful."

Kate looked at him. He was completely engrossed in what he was saying.

"I don't see why we can't do it here. We're about the same size as that college, and we certainly have the energy for it, with the students all keyed up by More Than Half a Brain."

"It sounds like a good idea," Kate said. She didn't even think of again confessing to being More Than Half a Brain. She had an idea of how to convince Sam of it, but it was still rather unformed.

"Will you help?" Sam asked. "I thought we could form a coalition between all the arts organizations on campus, and you certainly seem like the most appropriate person to represent the museum. As I remember it . . ."

Kate interrupted him before he could go any further. "Don't remember that."

"You mean the way you came tearing into my office that day and demanded that I reformulate my budget?" he teased. "Ah, Kate . . ." He took her hand and pressed it to his heart. "It's one of those moments I'll never forget. You were like an avenging angel."

Kate laughed and pulled her hand away. "And you—I thought you were an ogre. A mean-spirited penny pincher."

"And now?" He placed his hands on her shoulders

and held her at arm's length, searching her face for
whatever emotions it might betray.

"I think you care about the college. I think you
really want to help it get on its feet again." She paused.
"I'm sorry I ever doubted you."

"That's over and done with," Sam said as he dropped
his hands and continued to walk along the path.

A little voice in Kate's head piped up and said,
"No, it isn't." But she ignored the voice. Nothing was
going to mar her golden afternoon with Sam.

Chapter 11

THE WEEK HAD gone by so quickly that Kate could hardly believe it was Friday. She'd been busy with the exhibition—typing up the labels and printing the brochures, deciding on the final placement of the paintings, and organizing the little party afterward— and she'd barely had time to think of anything else. Her show of abstract expressionists was going to open in a little over a week. She was totally overwhelmed by all the details that had to be attended to.

After a week of almost utter chaos, she was surprised at how calm she was this afternoon. She felt exhilarated, with none of the underlying anxiety she had expected to feel. She knew her lack of anxiety must have something to do with Sam, because in spite of her preoccupation with her show, she had managed to spend a fair amount of time with him, and that seemed to have settled her nerves.

For some reason that neither of them could understand, the campus had been very quiet all week. There were no demonstrations, no mimeographed sheets pinned to tree trunks, and no students running around on fact-finding missions. Sam had told Kate that he found the quietness unsettling, since he knew the students were up to something. It bothered him that they were doing it in such a secretive fashion. But Kate found the lull a relief: It took the pressure off the inevitability of making Sam believe that she was the one who had started it all with her letter.

She was sitting at her desk, proofreading some labels, when Jane stuck her head in the door.

"The painters say they're done," she said. "They want you to come down and take a look."

Kate smiled to herself. Her precious painters—the ones she had never thought she'd be able to afford. They'd been hard at work all day long while she'd been holed up in her office, making phone calls and doing a million other things. Now she could finally see what they'd done.

"Come with me?" she asked Jane as she headed out the door.

"Okay. I haven't seen this yet either."

They went down to the main floor. A few of the painters, wearing paint-splattered white coveralls, were hanging around in front of the exhibition hall.

Strange, Kate thought. Why are all the spatters green?

She walked into the hall. The answer to her question was as plain as day. What she saw made her clutch her heart. The walls weren't off-white; they were green. Not the bilious green they'd been before, but green all the same.

"Oh, no," she moaned. "What happened?"

"Kate, the walls are green!" Jane said, as if Kate hadn't noticed it already.

"Who's in charge here?" Kate just managed to get out.

A sheepish-looking painter walked over and deposited himself in front of Kate. Obviously, he knew something was wrong, but he didn't look as if he knew exactly what it was. "I am," he said. "I'm Mario."

"Mario," Kate said calmly. The only way to deal with it, she told herself, was to stay calm. Don't get hysterical, she thought; there's plenty of time for that later. "These walls are green."

Mario scratched his head. "I know, miss. You asked for green."

Kate scanned his face for signs of mental derangement, but she couldn't find any. "No, I didn't. I asked for ivory."

"Ivy," he said. "You said ivy."

"Heaven help us!" Kate exclaimed, and rolled her eyes upward. "I most certainly did not. I asked for ivory. Off-white. It has nothing to do with green."

Mario pulled a pink slip out of his pocket. "But the requisition here says ivy."

"Let me see that." Kate nearly snatched the slip out of his hand. Sure enough, in a rather bold and flamboyant script was written *ivy*. "How could this have happened? I went to the paint store just to make sure I got the right color!" she wailed.

Jane sidled up next to her just in time to catch Kate's body as it began to crumple. She steadied her with one hand and gave Mario a commiserating look. "Well, we'll just have them paint over it."

Kate regained her composure and was able to stand without Jane's support. "Can you do that tomorrow?" she asked.

Mario shrugged his shoulders. "Sure. But it's time and a half on weekends."

Kate did some quick figuring in her head. "I don't have enough money for that, and it can't wait until

Monday. Those walls have to be dry by then."

"Weeeelll..." Jane remarked, squinching up her face. Mario's face, too, was puckered in thought.

Suddenly, Kate straightened up. Inspiration had struck. "We'll paint it ourselves."

Jane nodded. Mario nodded.

"I've got enough money left to buy the new paint. We'll do it tonight."

Jane looked less than thrilled.

"Did you have plans?" Kate asked. She hated to upset Jane's social life, but this was a full-fledged emergency.

"No, no," Jane said.

Kate suspected she was lying, but didn't press her. She needed her help too badly. She turned to Mario.

"Can you get me the amount of paint I'll need? Is it too late?"

Mario looked at his watch. "Naah. I'll run and get it. What color?"

"Ivory," Kate said as distinctly as possible. "Off-white, cream." She looked at him and smiled. "I know it's not your fault."

"Well, I'm sorry just the same," Mario said sincerely. "You'll need about five gallons. I'll go get 'em right now," he said, and then he was off.

An hour later, Kate and Jane were perched on ladders, stroking the walls with paint rollers. Several of the painters had felt so badly about the mixup that they had left their coveralls behind so Kate and Jane wouldn't have to run home and grab some old clothes. But the men hadn't left their hats, and already Kate's red hair had acquired white streaks. She hadn't realized what a messy business painting was.

"I've got an idea," Jane piped up as she was dipping her roller into the pan.

"What's that?"

"Why don't I go out and buy a couple bottles of wine? That'll make it a lot more fun."

Kate smiled at her. "Are you sure you can paint and drink at the same time?"

"Well, I know I can walk and chew gum at the same time, and this probably isn't much different." She headed for the door. "I'll be right back."

Kate continued to paint. Jane was right: With a little bit of wine in their systems, the work would probably be a lot more fun. Thank heavens Alex and Helen were out of town, visiting another museum. She'd hate to have them see what she'd been reduced to. But actually, when she thought about it, it was kind of funny, and she was sure that later, when the show was all over, the experience could be turned into an amusing anecdote that would cheer up another curator going through the last-minute hell of organizing a show. She could hear herself saying, "You think you've got it bad; well, I . . ." Kate laughed to herself just thinking about it.

"What's so funny, Kate?"

She turned quickly and almost fell off her ladder. It was Sam, with a very perplexed look on his face.

"I asked for ivory and I got ivy," Kate said.

"That makes sense," Sam admitted wryly. "I guess we're not having dinner, then."

Kate put a hand up to her face and slapped it lightly, realizing as she did that she was also slapping a white blush on her cheek. "I forgot all about dinner," she said apologetically.

"You look lovely in white," he said, coming up to her and giving her a quick peck on the cheek. "Are you sure you shouldn't have been a nurse?"

She laughed. "At this moment I wouldn't mind being a nurse, to tell you the truth."

"I guess you need some help."

"Would you?" Kate's eyes lit up. "Jane's coming back with some wine. We could turn it into a party."

"That sounds like fun!" Sam said, too exuberantly. Kate knew he was teasing her. "Well . . ."

"I can think of other things that would be even more fun." He leered at her with mock lecherousness.

Kate felt a rumbling in her veins. She had thought the feeling would begin to wear off, but it still reappeared whenever Sam looked at her in that certain way of his.

"Later," she said, laughing. "There's an extra pair of coveralls in the corner there, in case you don't want to look as if you've got a bad case of dandruff."

"I can tell already that this is going to be fun," Sam said heartily. "With a comedian, no less."

Jane returned with the wine, a corkscrew, and some plastic cups. Sam poured them each a cup of wine and made a humorous toast. Soon there was a festive air about the project. Jane even ran up to the office and brought down her radio so that they could listen to the college radio station. The disc jockey played an upbeat combination of rock, jazz, and disco.

Kate had finished one wall and was starting on another when the disc jockey came on the air and interrupted the music to make an announcement.

"We all know what's happening tomorrow, don't we?" he said, and then laughed.

Jane, Kate, and Sam all looked at each other.

"Don't forget: It starts at noon. Be there or be square." The music started up again.

Kate flashed a questioning look at Sam and he shrugged his bewilderment. Jane, on the other hand, continued to paint as if nothing had happened. She wouldn't meet Kate's eyes when Kate stared at her.

"Jane . . . ?" Kate asked tentatively.

"Yes?" Her face was the epitome of innocence.

"What was he talking about?"

"Oh, I don't know." Jane attacked the wall with her roller, painting as if her life depended on it.

Kate left her ladder and went to Jane's side. "You're holding out."

Jane looked up at her with a pleading look on her face. "I can't say," she whispered ferociously. *"He's* here." She tipped her head toward Sam.

Sam, who had been watching the two of them, came over.

"Is there a problem?" he asked.

Kate looked at him and laughed. Sam was having a hard time appearing authoritative in his coveralls. "Jane knows something, but she's not telling."

Sam looked at Jane and then held up his paint brush. Jane cowered like the guilty person she was. "Would you like to see what you look like with a white face?" he asked her, as if he were a gangster threatening to fit her feet with a pair of cement overshoes.

"No. I'll talk," Jane said, looking scared. "There's going to be a rally tomorrow."

A small moan escaped from Kate. So the lull had merely been the calm before the storm.

"Where?" Sam demanded.

Jane set down her paint roller. "I can't tell you that."

Sam advanced with the brush. "About that face of yours . . ." he said.

But Jane stood her ground. "I've been sworn to secrecy. Would you want me to break a solemn vow?" she asked.

Sam considered it and then lowered his brush. "No, I guess not. A person has to have some integrity." He thought for a moment. "But could you give me a clue?"

Jane looked at him and then smiled. "If you had more than half a brain, you'd know."

Sam laughed. Kate shifted on her feet nervously.

"Kate keeps telling me she's More Than Half a Brain," Sam said.

Kate laughed uneasily. Jane just stood there, chewing her lip. Did she know? Kate wondered.

"Well, you'll find out tomorrow," Jane said vaguely, and she went back to painting.

Sam looked at Kate, shrugged, and started painting again himself.

"Are my eyes deceiving me?" Helen Drummond stood in the entrance to the gallery with her coat on and her arms full of books.

"Helen!" Kate exclaimed. "What are you doing here?"

Helen smiled. "I guess I could ask you the same question."

"The painters made a mistake and now we're correcting it," Kate said.

"And putting to rest all those nasty rumors about how art historians study art because they themselves can't paint," Helen joked. "I just wanted to drop off these books that I got on my trip with Alex before I went home. But as long as you're here, Kate, can you take a break? There's something I want to show you."

Kate looked down at her paint-splattered coveralls. "I'd probably get whatever it is a little messy. Can it wait?"

"No," Helen said firmly. "Come up to my office with me."

Kate observed Helen. She looked as if she had something on her mind and wasn't going to be put off by any excuses. "All right," she said, and followed her colleague to the elevator.

"How's Sam?" Helen asked on their way up.

"He's fine," Kate answered.

"Have you told him?" Helen looked very concerned.

Kate nodded. "But he refuses to believe me."

Helen scrutinized her closely. "Why?"

Kate thought about that for a moment. "I'm not exactly sure. Maybe he just doesn't want to."

"Maybe he has a reason not to want to," Helen said knowingly as they stepped off the elevator. "Have you thought about that?"

They walked through empty galleries and climbed the staircase at the end of the last one. When they got to Helen's office, she threw her armload of books down on her desk, snapped on a light, and invited Kate to sit. Helen sat behind her desk, looking grim.

"You don't really want to show me anything, do you, Helen?" Kate asked her, feeling an uneasy premonition.

"No. But I do want to tell you something. I had a long talk with Alex today about this and we both agreed that you should know."

"What is it?"

"It's about your donor. We know who it is."

"Is it Sam?"

"Sam didn't put up the money. Chilton Harrison did. He told me at the meeting last week."

Now Kate knew why Harrison had been so friendly with her the week before. She had been so busy lately that she hadn't had a chance to ponder his behavior and figure out what it was all about. "Is there something wrong with that?" she asked.

"Well," Helen said, "it seems as if a certain college president asked him, as a personal favor, to make the donation."

"Oh." Kate supposed she should be angry, but she wasn't. Strange.

"I just thought you should know"—Helen gave her a piercing glance—"before you get too involved."

"I already am too involved," Kate said with a smile.

"You don't seem upset."

"Well, I'm not. You see, that happened before I got to know Sam, but even so, I don't think he meant any harm by it. I think he just wanted to help."

Helen looked surprised, and then she seemed to understand. "You really love Sam, don't you?"

Kate smiled. "What's even more important is that I trust him."

"I'd hoped you'd feel this way, but I wasn't sure. After . . ."

Kate knew exactly what she was going to say. "David Atwood was a long time ago, and he was a different type of man. Besides, I can't really be angry with Sam for doing something that I did myself."

"You mean the anonymous letter?"

"Yes. I guess we kind of balance each other out."

"But you tried to tell him," Helen reminded her.

Kate hadn't thought about that. "He'll tell me."

"You sound really sure." Helen was smiling.

Kate smiled back. "Just between us, Helen, I've learned a really important lesson since I meant Sam."

Helen raised her eyebrows.

Kate continued. "I thought that falling in love meant losing control of your life. I thought that when you gave your heart to someone, it meant that you lost it. But that's not how it works at all."

"How does it work?" Helen asked. She looked as if she really wanted to know.

"You get strength from it. When you trust enough to give your heart, it's as though you gain a kind of faith, not just in yourself, but in everything. Now I know that I can do whatever I want. I'm not afraid anymore—of myself, or life, or even of failing. When I gave my heart to Sam, that's what I got in return. And the most wonderful part of it is that I wasn't expecting that to happen at all. It just did."

Helen came around to where Kate was sitting and gave her a big hug. "I'm so glad you feel that way. I was afraid that I'd be giving you bad news."

Kate hugged her back. "Not a chance."

"Shall we go back down?" Helen asked.

"Sure," Kate said, and then flashed Helen a devilish look. "Would you like to help?"

"I've got to go home and see if my husband's been fed yet," Helen explained as they left her office. "A hungry husband takes precedence over green walls. Agreed?"

Kate nodded her head. "Agreed."

When they got back down to the gallery, Sam was painting alone.

"Jane went home. I said it was okay."

"I think she had a date," Kate said ruefully. "Maybe she can at least catch half of it." She looked at her watch. It was almost midnight.

Helen said her good-byes and then Sam and Kate were left alone in the gallery with one more wall to paint.

"What did Helen show you?" Sam asked.

"I think I showed her something," Kate said, more to herself than Sam.

"Oh?" Sam had a puzzled look on his face.

"You had to be there," Kate replied playfully.

"I wish I had been," Sam said. "I don't like being apart from you, Katie." He gazed over at her from where he was at the other end of the wall.

Kate felt as if she didn't even have to get up and go toward him. The intensity of his gaze seemed almost enough to draw her to his side.

"I don't like it either," she said when she was standing next to him. She was surprised at how forthright she was able to be with him. It seemed like such a long time ago when she didn't trust him, or the feelings she had for him. It felt as if that had been another life completely.

"Well," Sam said as he wrapped his arms around her, "there are ways of fixing that." His lips found hers and they were soft and warm and inviting, promising many wonderful delights.

"Not until this wall is done," she reproved him, and tapped him softly with the end of her paint roller.

"Slave driver," he mumbled as he began to paint again.

"Have some wine," Kate said. "That should improve your mood."

Several hours later, they were done. Tired, and slightly tipsy from all the wine they'd drunk, they stumbled out of the museum. It was so late that they could see the faintest tinge of dawn sneaking up into the eastern sky. Kate was resting her head on Sam's shoulder as they walked, and Sam was leaning against Kate. Leaves scuttled along the sidewalk, making dry, scratching noises, but everything else was quiet. Havenport lay asleep all around them.

"Where's your car?" Kate mumbled sleepily.

"Home," Sam said.

They reached the corner. Kate turned to head toward her apartment. "I guess it's not too far to walk."

Sam grabbed her by the arm and steered her in the opposite direction. "Tonight we stay at my house."

The president's house! "Is it appropriate?" she asked.

"Appropriate!" Sam exclaimed. "I should say so. I think it's entirely appropriate for the woman the president loves to keep him company at his humble abode."

"'Humble abode' isn't exactly how I'd describe it," Kate contradicted him. "'Gilded splendor' is more like it."

"Whatever." He tugged her firmly along the sidewalk. "You're coming with me."

In a few minutes, they were heading up the hill that led to the president's house. Perched on the crest of a long, grassy incline, its front lawn was large enough to contain a croquet game and a badminton tournament simultaneously, which actually happened in the spring. The house itself was a Georgian brick, ivy-covered mansion. The windows were shuttered in white and the roof had copper detailing, a later addition that had oxidized to a pale, sea green. The college maintained it meticulously, since it was a landmark of sorts; every year it appeared on the cover of the college catalog.

A simple brick staircase led up to the front door, and Sam resolutely piloted Kate up the stairs. She didn't exactly know how she felt about going there with Sam. It would be a little bit like spending the night in a museum.

"Are you scared?" he asked gently.

"Well, not exactly," she lied.

"But this is where I live," Sam said, opening the door.

"This is where the president lives," Kate replied.

"Well, Katie, you know I'm the president."

"I know, but I've gotten used to you as just being Sam." She paused in the doorway.

"But I'm Radley, too, you know. You'd better get used to that." He took her hand tenderly and drew her into the house.

Up until then neither Sam nor Kate had mentioned a word about the future of their relationship; there had been too much for both of them to do to think about it. But now, Kate realized, Sam was trying to tell her something with his gentle admonition. "I should?" she asked quietly.

"Yes, you should," he said firmly. "And there's something else you're going to have to get used to, too." He grasped a lock of her hair in his fingers and rolled it between them as if it were a strand of fine gold.

Kate looked up into his eyes. Would she ever get used to his fiery glance? "What's that?" she murmured.

"How love-starved I am." And with that, Sam picked her up and began to carry her up the stairs to his bedroom.

Kate laughed. It was a sound of pure joy.

Chapter 12

PANDEMONIUM. THAT WAS Kate's first impression as she awoke. There was an awful lot of noise going on somewhere, and it sounded as if it were in Sam's front yard. Sam still lay sleeping next to her, his arm thrown possessively across her waist.

Slowly she extricated herself from his hold. She grabbed her sweater, which was draped over a chair near the bed, and pulled it on quickly. Then she went over to the window, pushed aside the curtain, and looked out. What she saw made her heart stop in her chest.

Pandemonium was probably the most apt description of what was going on in front of the president's house. The lawn was filled with students—students who must have had an appreciable amount of beer in their stomachs, judging from the kegs scattered among them. Some of them were carrying the same placards they had waved around at last weekend's rally, and the marching band and the cheerleaders were lining up behind them.

So this was where they had decided to hold their rally! If only Sam had been more persuasive with Jane when she had refused to tell him where it was going to be, Kate thought. Now she was trapped.

She looked over at Sam. He was still asleep, a wonder, considering the decibel level of the throng outside. Now what was she going to do? She had to get out of the president's house without being seen.

Something told Kate that the jig was up. But even if she didn't feel that way, discretion alone would have been enough of an excuse to get her out of the house and away from the unruly hordes outside, pronto. It wouldn't do to have the whole school know that she was leaving President Davis's house in the morning. The conclusions that would be drawn would be the right ones. Like a flash of lightning, Kate slipped on her skirt, stockings, and shoes. She prayed that Sam would stay asleep until she got out the door. She knew she was taking the cowardly way out, but she was so panic-stricken that she didn't even stop to question her motives. As soon as she had slipped her second shoe on, she raced to the door of Sam's bedroom, but it wasn't soon enough. Just as she reached the hallway, she heard his voice calling her name, and then it was swallowed up by a tremendous roar from outside.

"Come out, come out!" she heard the crowd roar. "Come out, President Davis!"

Kate ran down the central staircase and saw the front door, situated between two organza-curtained windows. Beyond the windows was a crowd of students that looked even larger up close than it had appeared from the second story. Escaping through the front door was out of the question.

She turned and ran toward the back of the house and found herself in the kitchen. She peeked out a window over the sink and saw that the back lawn was clear; everything was happening out front. All she had to do to make her escape a secret was somehow get from the backyard to the side yard and away without being detected.

She opened the kitchen door and slipped out. Just as she hit the back steps, the band, out front, slammed into a rousing version of "The Stripper." She didn't have time to figure that one out; she just headed over to her right, where, she hoped, a cluster of trees and shrubbery would conceal her movements as she snuck away. Unfortunately, luck wasn't with her.

Just as she was about to reach the cover of the first evergreen, an obviously inebriated couple came swerving out of the shrubbery and headed straight at her. Before Kate could avoid them, they took one of her arms and began to drag her to the front of the house.

"You've gotta see this, you've gotta see this," the male component of the twosome babbled. "They're gonna unmask More Than Half a Brain!"

But how could that be? Nobody had bothered to tell her! Kate let herself be dragged along, too stunned to protest.

The front lawn was a mass of gyrating bodies. The band had just gotten to the bump and grind part of "The Stripper," and the crowd was taking it literally. Several young girls looked as if they were about to dislocate their hips, and the cheerleaders were tossing their pom-poms about with abandon. Above the noise of the band, Kate could hear a group of students chanting for President Davis's appearance. If he didn't come out soon, Kate knew, chaos would break loose. Just as the band launched into its second number, "The Great Pretender," the front door of the president's house opened and Sam stood on the front steps, his hair tousled and his attire in a general state of dishevelment.

The crowd quieted down, obviously waiting to hear what Sam had to say.

"Good morning!" he yelled, as if being awakened by a roaring crowd was something that happened to him all the time.

"Good morning!" they roared back.

"This is some party," he said, smoothing his hair. "But next time, send me an invitation!"

Everyone laughed. One brave soul yelled out, "We were afraid you wouldn't come."

Sam laughed. "Well, I'm here now. To what do I owe this outstanding honor?"

A young man separated himself from the crowd, which was completely silent as he approached the front steps. "President Davis," he said, "on this auspicious occasion, I have the great pleasure to present to you that person for whom we all have the greatest respect, someone who speaks for all of us here at Havenport." He paused. The crowd seemed to be holding its collective breath until he spoke again.

He turned and gestured to the back of the gathering. "I present to you, President Davis, More Than Half a Brain!" The band kicked into "Hail to the Chief." In a moment as magical as when Moses parted the Red Sea, the crowd separated into two halves and down the middle of it marched—oh, how could it be? Kate thought—Jane Fedders, looking as terrified as it was possible for a young woman to look. Half the crowd booed and the other half cheered, but before she could even think twice, Kate heard herself shouting "Wait!"

Kate had never known what it was like to be the center of attention, but now, as all eyes were upon her, she suddenly understood what stage fright was all about. Her stomach fluttered with a thousand butterflies straining to be let loose, and her heart pounded like the kettle drums booming in the back of the band. She snaked through the crowd until she was standing in front of Jane.

Jane had a look of triumph on her face. Sotto voce, she whispered to Kate. "I knew it was you."

"You were right," Kate whispered back. "Now what do I do?"

Jane laughed. "Tell Sam. This time, trust me, he'll believe you."

Kate waited until the crowd had quieted down and then announced in a surprisingly loud voice, "I am More Than Half a Brain!"

The crowd went wild. Someone shoved a plastic cup filled with beer into her hand and she downed it with one quick twist of her wrist. This wasn't going to be easy. Suddenly, she felt herself being lifted up onto someone's shoulders and carried to the front step of the president's house.

Kate looked up. Sam was standing on the landing with his arms crossed over his chest. His face held an expression that Kate found indecipherable. Was he angry? Was he relieved? Or was he just waiting to see how she was going to get herself out of the mess she'd gotten herself into?

"President Davis," she began, "I think we have what you might call a lack of communication here."

The crowd roared. Kate was surprised at how easily she was seizing command of the situation.

"We all want Havenport to remain the great college

we know it is." Kate felt the fellow whose shoulders she was hoisted upon begin to tremble beneath her weight. "Could you please put me down?" she asked.

He let her down. The crowd applauded. Was there nothing she could say that wouldn't be greeted with cheers? Kate cleared her throat and continued. "But I speak for all of us when I say that we're disturbed by your budget cuts."

The crowd agreed with many shouts of "Right" and "Right on."

What was she going to say next? Kate began to panic, but then an idea came to her. She remembered what Sam had said last Sunday about initiating a fund-raising drive that the whole school could participate in. But instead of suggesting it herself, she felt it was only right to let Sam be the one to set it in motion. It was his brainstorm, and the students of Havenport should know that he wasn't afraid to change his mind about something if he found out there was a better way of doing it.

She threw the ball into his court. "What can we do about this?"

Kate looked straight at Sam and smiled. Finally, he reacted to her. He smiled back. He knew what she was up to.

"Funny that you should ask that, More Than Half a Brain," he said.

The crowd roared with laughter. Kate joined in, half hysterical with relief. He wasn't angry with her— he truly wasn't.

Sam continued. "I have an idea."

"What is it? What is it?" the crowd asked.

"Will you help me with it?" he inquired.

"Yes! Yes!" they responded with a great deal of enthusiasm.

"Then let's start a fund drive. Does anyone have some ideas about how we can raise money?"

"Cake sales!" one coed yelled. "Car washes," another added. "Holding professors hostage!" a rather zealous young man suggested, to much good-natured laughter.

Sam nodded his head. "I can see you have all kinds of ideas. Why don't we hold a meeting on Monday to discuss them?" He walked down the stairs, grasped Kate's hand in his own, and pulled her back up with him. "And you," he said, his eyes twinkling, "you, More Than Half a Brain, are going to have to prove what you claim with your name. I'm putting you in charge of this motley crew." The crowd laughed, delighted with Sam's description of them.

"You are going to form a committee for me with representatives from all four classes." He looked out at the crowd. "Any volunteers?"

Everyone waved their hands about wildly and charged toward the front steps. Kate clung to Sam, just for a moment, and then went down to meet her fans. They picked her up bodily, dozens of hands working together to keep her up in the air, and then another group did the same to Sam.

As she bounced on the palms of her well-wishers, Kate yelled over at Sam, "I told you so!"

Sam looked as if he were having his own problems trying to stay balanced on the upstretched hands of a dozen or so somewhat inebriated students. He merely laughed.

* * *

"Well, I hate to say it again, but I'll say it again," Kate said. "I told you so."

She and Sam were slouching on her couch, recovering from an afternoon that would have put a less hardy couple under for good. After they'd been paraded all around campus on the shoulders of their admirers, they were the guests of honor at several impromptu student parties, where the beer flowed fast and furiously and one wild dance followed another. Caught up in the mood, Kate had danced, too, and now her aching calves and shoulders were making her regret her high spirits.

A tray of nibbled cheese and crackers and two drained coffee cups lay on the coffee table. Why was sobering up such a grim process?

She reached over and tickled Sam in the ribs. "I told you so," she repeated in a singsong chant.

He grabbed her wrist. "Listen, Kate, you are being perfectly obnoxious about this whole thing."

"I tried to tell you," she reminded him. "But would you listen? No!" She went in for the attack, tickling him mercilessly.

"Stop. Stop it, Kate, right now." Sam's face wasn't jolly anymore. In fact, he looked upset.

He held on to her hands until he was sure that she had gotten his message. "Okay," she said. "I'll stop."

Sam sank even lower into the couch and rested his hand against his brow. Kate leaned over and took the hand away, cradling it in her own hand instead. His eyes met hers and they seemed very sad.

"What's wrong?" she asked.

He looked away and then began to speak. "You've been trying to tell me something and I wouldn't listen."

"That's all right," Kate said. "I don't mind your thinking that I wasn't More Than Half a Brain. I mean, she's a little far out, isn't she?"

Sam smiled wanly. "That's not exactly it."

Kate thought she knew what "it" was, but she didn't want to prod him to tell her. That was something he had to decide to do himself.

He pulled her hand out of her lap, where it had been comforting his, and clutched it tightly against his chest. "I have my own confession to make."

Kate didn't know whether to pretend that she didn't know what he was referring to, or admit that she did. She said nothing.

"You know that anonymous donation?" His eyes probed hers with golden intensity.

She nodded.

"I talked Chilton Harrison into it. I asked him to do it as a personal favor to me." His words came out stilted and slow. "And I asked him to donate it anonymously so there was no possibility of your tracing it back to me."

"I know," Kate said softly. "I know all about that."

Sam sat up quickly. "You know! And you're not angry?"

Kate turned to him. "Were you angry when you found out that I was really More Than Half a Brain?"

"No," Sam said. "But that's different."

"How is it different?"

"Don't you think that I was trying to compromise you?"

"Well," Kate said slowly, "don't you think that I was trying to trip you up?"

Sam looked at her, puzzled, and then a spark of understanding seemed to ignite in his eyes. "I guess we've both been up to no good, haven't we?"

"Yes, I guess so," Kate agreed, moving next to him and putting his arm around her shoulder. "But there's something funny about it."

He stroked her arm absentmindedly as he pondered what she had said. "What's that?"

"We're just no good at being no good."

Sam chuckled.

"It's the truth. I tried to make things tough for you with that letter of mine, but instead I helped you figure out how to save the college."

Now Sam caught on. "And I was bullheaded about not giving you the money for your show, then got it for you anonymously and risked the wrath of a compromised curator, who now tells me she doesn't feel compromised at all." He touched her cheek lightly with the tips of his fingers. "Why's that, Katie?"

She shivered beneath his touch. "Because I know you had no intention of compromising me."

"No, I didn't," he whispered.

"But I also knew something else."

He cocked his head.

"I knew that whether I had the money or not, I'd make a success of that show. Because the money wasn't really the problem. The problem was that I didn't have any faith in myself." She gulped and went on. "Until I met you."

"Well," Sam said softly, "I'll be damned." His face shone with pride. "Is that what I did?"

"Yes," she replied seriously. "And something else."

He chucked her under the chin. "Stop, you're giving me a big head."

"You saved me from being an old maid."

Sam drew away from her and laughed as if he'd

never stop. Every time he took a look at her he began to laugh again, until finally Kate looked so miffed that he must have known he was in danger of seriously offending her.

"I'm sorry, Katie, but the thought of you as an old maid..." He stopped talking and scooped her up in his arms. His mouth touched hers.

Kate did what she always did: She kissed him back with all the desire and love she felt for him.

Sam let her go after a minute or so. "Well," he said, "anyone who kisses like that is in no danger of being an old maid, Katie."

"But it's only because I'm kissing you," she insisted.

"That kiss was always there, Katie. It was always inside of you. All you had to do was let it out."

"You make it sound as if you have nothing to do with it. Maybe I should kiss every man I meet like that."

He reached over and tugged her fiercely toward him. "I wouldn't advise that," he said as his lips met hers.

"Why not?" she mumbled hotly against him.

"You wouldn't want to be responsible for putting a man in jail, would you?"

"You'd put him in jail?" she asked. She didn't think that a college president's powers extended that far.

Sam heaved an exasperated sigh. "No, my adorably dense Kate. I'd be in jail for bopping him on the nose."

"I don't think I'll kiss anyone else, then," Kate said as Sam's lips hovered above her own, on the brink of lowering and claiming her mouth.

"A wise decision, Katie."

Then a thought occurred to her. She shifted slightly

and moved her mouth away so that Sam's lips grazed her cheek. "What about you?" she asked.

"Oh," he said, pulling her back into kissing range, "I have no intention of kissing anyone else. More Than Half a Brain is more than enough for me."

The gallery was jammed. It was the opening night of Kate's exhibit.

"I can't believe how many people are here!" she whispered to Sam.

"Well, you have achieved a bit of notoriety in these parts," he whispered back.

Kate laughed. Apparently, what he said was true. The campus controversy had made all the local newspapers, and it seemed that not only the students and faculty of Havenport had showed up, but a good portion of the townspeople had, too, just to see what More Than Half a Brain had done.

Alex approached. He looked very happy. "Kate," he said with his hand extended, "congratulations are in order." He shook her hand.

Kate leaned over and kissed him on the cheek. "Thanks, Alex. I couldn't have done it without your support."

Alex pooh-poohed her expression of gratitude. "I had nothing to do with it. You did it all yourself."

Sam cleared his throat. "With a little help..."

Alex gave him a sly look. "Ah, yes, the anonymous donor."

"We all know whom we have to thank for that." Kate beamed a happy smile at Sam and clasped his hand in hers.

"Yes. Me." It was Chilton Harrison.

"That's right," Kate said, kissing Harrison quickly

on the cheek. "I haven't had a chance to thank you properly yet."

Harrison blushed. "It took a bit of persuasion from this young man here"—he laid a hand on Sam's shoulder—"but I can see now that he was right when he told me I'd be backing a winner."

Now it was Kate's turn to blush. Was that how Sam had described her to Harrison? He had known all along that she'd pull the exhibition off. He'd had faith in her from the very beginning.

"It's beautiful, Kate." Helen Drummond had broken through the crowd. Kate gave her a light peck on the cheek. "And it's so modernistic, so spare." Helen winked, and then both she and Kate burst into giggles. Only they knew that if the effect was spare and modernistic, it was more from economics than aesthetics.

"Here's to minimalism," Kate said, and raised her plastic glass full of wine.

Everyone followed suit.

"And here's to Havenport," Sam said. They raised their glasses even higher and then drank heartily.

"Speaking of which..." Alex said. He nudged Kate in the ribs. "Have you told the president yet?"

Kate nearly choked on her wine. She'd been so busy, she'd completely forgotten.

Sam eyed her suspiciously.

"Don't look at me like that," she pleaded. "This is good news."

His handsome face broke into a smile, and Kate's heart pounded in her chest at the sight of it. She supposed that Sam's smile would never lose the power to make her heart jump for joy.

"Kate found something in an attic," Alex prompted her.

"That's right, my thrift-shop days stood me in good stead." She was teasing Sam by being slow about telling him the news.

"Well . . . go on!" Obviously, his patience was wearing thin.

"Remember that man, Mr. Winthrop, who said he had a chest in his attic? Well, I went to see him last week." She stopped.

"And what did you find?" Sam prodded her.

"The chest itself wasn't much. Just an old cedar hope chest."

"But never one to leave a stone unturned . . ." Alex put in.

"I opened it up. I thought at least there might be some clothing in it we could use for the costume institute."

"But it wasn't clothing," Alex said excitedly.

"Nope," Kate went on. "It was another old chest, only this one was smaller and made of oak."

"Will you get to the point?" Sam said. "All we're doing is opening chests. What did you find, Katie?"

"A complete set of old Tiffany silver, including the tea service, in the original oak chest. It's a beautiful chrysanthemum pattern from the turn of the century."

"That's nice," Sam said, still not understanding what all the fuss was about. "Winthrop ought to make a pretty penny from that."

"That's just the point," Kate said, the excitement finally bubbling over so that her words rushed out of her mouth. "Mr. Winthrop didn't even know the silver was there, and he said that he never would have known it was there if it hadn't been for me, so he gave the silver to the museum."

"Great," Sam said. "Good work, Kate." He patted her on the back.

"But that's not it!" She was really in the mood of the thing now. "We don't have to keep it."

Now Sam was exasperated with her. "Of course we'll keep it," he said firmly.

"No, we won't. Winthrop says it's all right if we auction it. Do you know how much that service will bring at auction?"

"A lot?" Sam asked.

"A whole lot," Kate answered. "And do you know where the money is going?"

"No," Sam said, but Kate had a feeling that he had a good idea.

"It's going to be the first donation to the Havenport College Endowment Fund," she said proudly. "What do you think of that?"

Everyone looked at Sam, wondering what his reaction would be. He stroked his chin slowly, as if he really had to consider what he thought. Then his face broke into the widest grin Kate had ever seen, and, right in front of everyone, he swept her up into his arms.

"I think it's great!" he exclaimed as he kissed her loudly.

"Sam!" Kate said, struggling in his arms. "What will people think?" she whispered in his ear.

Sam pulled back and stared straight into her eyes. Oh, no, Kate thought, here we go again. "They'll think I love you and they'll be right."

"Hear, hear," said Alex, raising his glass.

"Long live More Than Half a Brain," teased Helen, joining Alex in his toast.

But Kate hardly heard them. All she was aware of

was Sam's eyes, blazing like autumn bonfires as he gazed at her lovingly. Her heart felt so full of love for him that it seemed to have expanded and filled up her whole chest. She barely managed to squeak out her question. "Do you? Do you really love me?" she whispered so that only he could hear.

He cocked his head to one side and sighed with exasperation, but his arms still held her close, and through the tweedy fabric of his jacket she could feel his heart thumping along companionably with her own. "Would you like it in writing?" he asked, and gave her a little shake as if to bring her back to her senses.

"No, no," she murmured. "I think we've had our fill of letter-writing for the time being." She looked down at her feet, suddenly very much aware that everyone was staring at her and Sam. But the funny thing was, she didn't really care.

"How about if it's written on a marriage license?" Sam asked. He placed a hand underneath her chin and brought her face up so that she was forced to look into his eyes. The bonfires had turned into a flaming conflagration. "Will you marry me, Kate?"

Kate heard the swift intake of several people's breaths. She'd never expected to be proposed to in the middle of a crowd, but it gave the event a distinct air of high drama. There was a hush, as if everyone were waiting eagerly for her answer. Including Sam.

But that little devil, who always popped up in her mind at the most inopportune moments, was waving his miniature pitchfork around and demanding to be heard. She listened, smiled, and then asked her own question.

"Which one is asking? Radley or Sam?" She looked directly into his eyes as she asked, and the intensity of his gaze made her crack a nervous smile. Perhaps she really was playing with fire this time. Sam looked so serious, so determined, she knew that he didn't want any obstacles put in his way.

"Whichever one you want, darling." He arched an eyebrow and looked at her playfully. "But why not take both?"

She gave him a long, measuring look. That little devil was really pressing his luck this time. "I think I *will* take both," she answered boldly.

"Think you can handle 'em?" Sam asked slyly.

Kate heard several people in the crowd try to stifle their laughter, and she found it difficult to keep a straight face herself.

"I think so," she replied. "After all, I've got more than half a brain, haven't I?"

Sam drew her into his arms and kissed her roughly, passionately, as if his whole life depended upon it. The kiss left her breathless but not weak; she felt utterly exhilarated. While his lips were still pressed against hers, she almost felt, rather than heard, his reply.

"Much more, darling, much more than that, but we'll discuss it later."

She looked up into his eyes, basking in their warm, golden glow. And then Sam winked, giving her the distinct impression that their "discussion" would be a bit more than just the mere exchange of words. But they had a whole lifetime together to explore all the different meanings of Sam's wink, and that was exactly what Kate Burnham intended to do.

WONDERFUL ROMANCE NEWS!

Do you know about the exciting SECOND CHANCE AT LOVE/TO HAVE AND TO HOLD newsletter? Are you on our *free* mailing list? If reading all about your favorite authors, getting sneak previews of their latest releases, and being filled in on all the latest happenings and events in the romance world sounds good to you, then you'll love our SECOND CHANCE AT LOVE and TO HAVE AND TO HOLD Romance News.

If you'd like to be added to our mailing list, just fill out the coupon below and send it in…and we'll send you your *free* newsletter every three months — hot off the press.

☐ *Yes, I would like to receive your free SECOND CHANCE AT LOVE/TO HAVE AND TO HOLD newsletter.*

Name _____

Address _____

City _____ **State/Zip** _____

Please return this coupon to:

    Berkley Publishing
    200 Madison Avenue, New York, New York 10016
    Att: Irene Majuk

Second Chance at Love.

_____ 07595-7	RECKLESS DESIRE #180	Nicola Andrews
_____ 07596-5	THE RUSHING TIDE #181	Laura Eaton
_____ 07597-3	SWEET TRESPASS #182	Diana Mars
_____ 07598-1	TORRID NIGHTS #183	Beth Brookes
_____ 07800-X	WINTERGREEN #184	Jeanne Grant
_____ 07801-8	NO EASY SURRENDER #185	Jan Mathews
_____ 07802-6	IRRESISTIBLE YOU #186	Claudia Bishop
_____ 07803-4	SURPRISED BY LOVE #187	Jasmine Craig
_____ 07804-2	FLIGHTS OF FANCY #188	Linda Barlow
_____ 07805-0	STARFIRE #189	Lee Williams
_____ 07806-9	MOONLIGHT RHAPSODY #190	Kay Robbins
_____ 07807-7	SPELLBOUND #191	Kate Nevins
_____ 07808-5	LOVE THY NEIGHBOR #192	Frances Davies
_____ 07809-3	LADY WITH A PAST #193	Elissa Curry
_____ 07810-7	TOUCHED BY LIGHTNING #194	Helen Carter
_____ 07811-5	NIGHT FLAME #195	Sarah Crewe
_____ 07812-3	SOMETIMES A LADY #196	Jocelyn Day
_____ 07813-1	COUNTRY PLEASURES #197	Lauren Fox
_____ 07814-X	TOO CLOSE FOR COMFORT #198	Liz Grady
_____ 07815-8	KISSES INCOGNITO #199	Christa Merlin
_____ 07816-6	HEAD OVER HEELS #200	Nicola Andrews
_____ 07817-4	BRIEF ENCHANTMENT #201	Susanna Collins
_____ 07818-2	INTO THE WHIRLWIND #202	Laurel Blake
_____ 07819-0	HEAVEN ON EARTH #203	Mary Haskell
_____ 07820-4	BELOVED ADVERSARY #204	Thea Frederick
_____ 07821-2	SEASWEPT #205	Maureen Norris
_____ 07822-0	WANTON WAYS #206	Katherine Granger
_____ 07823-9	A TEMPTING MAGIC #207	Judith Yates
_____ 07956-1	HEART IN HIDING #208	Francine Rivers
_____ 07957-X	DREAMS OF GOLD AND AMBER #209	Robin Lynn
_____ 07958-8	TOUCH OF MOONLIGHT #210	Liz Grady
_____ 07959-6	ONE MORE TOMORROW #211	Aimée Duvall
_____ 07960-X	SILKEN LONGINGS #212	Sharon Francis
_____ 07961-8	BLACK LACE AND PEARLS #213	Elissa Curry

All of the above titles are $1.95
Prices may be slightly higher in Canada.
